You won't want to miss any of the memorable characters in this newest series by bestselling author Lass Small. While each of THE KEEPERS OF TEXAS books stands on its own, the continuing saga of the Keeper family and ranch will surely keep you coming back for more!

CAST OF CHARACTERS

Rip Morris: This stubborn and seductive cowboy worked hard for the Keeper family. And though he had a reputation as a ladies' man, he'd only reveal his true nature to one special lady. Could she be…

Lu Parsons: This innocent Texas socialite was going to learn more about the birds and the bees than she ever dreamed. And maybe she'd find a permanent home on the Keeper ranch, though she'd only come to town to take care of her brother…

Andrew Parsons: What had this greenhorn been doing, trespassing on Keeper land? And what would he remember once he awoke from his unconscious state? One person was determined to uncover the truth about the mysterious accident….

Tom Keeper: Heir to the Keeper ranch, he'd loved and lost one time too many. He claimed to have given up any thoughts of marriage, but Mrs. Right could be just around the corner!

Dear Reader,

This month Silhouette Desire brings you six brand-new, emotional and sensual novels by some of the bestselling— and most beloved—authors in the romance genre. Cait London continues her hugely popular miniseries THE TALLCHIEFS with *The Seduction of Fiona Tallchief,* April's MAN OF THE MONTH. Next, Elizabeth Bevarly concludes her BLAME IT ON BOB series with *The Virgin and the Vagabond.* And when a socialite confesses her virginity to a cowboy, she just might be *Taken by a Texan,* in Lass Small's THE KEEPERS OF TEXAS miniseries.

Plus, we have Maureen Child's *Maternity Bride, The Cowboy and the Calendar Girl,* the last in the OPPOSITES ATTRACT series by Nancy Martin, and Kathryn Taylor's tale of domesticating an office-bound hunk in *Taming the Tycoon.*

I hope you enjoy all six of Silhouette Desire's selections this month—and every month!

Regards,

Melissa Senate

Senior Editor
Silhouette Books

Please address questions and book requests to:
Silhouette Reader Service
U.S.: 3010 Walden Ave., P.O. Box 1325, Buffalo, NY 14269
Canadian: P.O. Box 609, Fort Erie, Ont. L2A 5X3

LASS SMALL
TAKEN BY A TEXAN

SILHOUETTE *Desire*®
Published by Silhouette Books
America's Publisher of Contemporary Romance

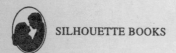

SILHOUETTE BOOKS

ISBN 0-373-76137-6

TAKEN BY A TEXAN

Copyright © 1998 by Lass Small

This edition published by arrangement with Harlequin Books S.A.

® and TM are trademarks of Harlequin Books S.A., used under license. Trademarks indicated with ® are registered in the United States Patent and Trademark Office, the Canadian Trade Marks Office and in other countries.

Printed in U.S.A.

Books by Lass Small

Silhouette Desire

Tangled Web #241
To Meet Again #322
Stolen Day #341
Possibles #356
Intrusive Man #373
To Love Again #397
Blindman's Bluff #413
Goldilocks and the Behr #437
Hide and Seek #453
Red Rover #491
Odd Man Out #505
Tagged #534
Contact #548
Wrong Address, Right Place #569
Not Easy #578
The Loner #594
Four Dollars and Fifty-One Cents #613
No Trespassing Allowed #638
The Molly Q #655
†*'Twas the Night* #684
Dominic #697
†*A Restless Man* #731
†*Two Halves* #743
†*Beware of Widows* #755
A Disruptive Influence #775
†*Balanced* #800
†*Tweed* #817
†*A New Year* #830
†*I'm Gonna Get You* #848
†*Salty and Felicia* #860
†*Lemon* #879
†*An Obsolete Man* #895
A Nuisance #901
Impulse #926
Whatever Comes #963
My House or Yours? #974

A Stranger in Texas #994
The Texas Blue Norther #1027
The Coffeepot Inn #1045
Chancy's Cowboy #1064
How To Win (Back) a Wife #1107
‡*Taken by a Texan* #1137

Silhouette Romance

An Irritating Man #444
Snow Bird #521

Silhouette Yours Truly

Not Looking for a Texas Man
*The Case of the Lady in
Apartment 308*

Silhouette Books

Silhouette Christmas Stories 1989
"Voice of the Turtles"
Silhouette Spring Fancy 1993
"Chance Encounter"

*Lambert Series
†Fabulous Brown Brothers
‡ The Keepers of Texas

LASS SMALL

finds living on this planet at this time a fascinating experience. People are amazing. She thinks that to be a teller of tales of people, places and things is absolutely marvelous.

Prologue

It all began, oddly enough, because Thomas Keeper was a restless man who had been overlooked by the female gender. Of course he was also a selective man, and had limited the opposite gender to those females who attracted him.

Tom was a TEXAS man. Which meant that he wasn't something as simple as just male. He thought like a man. He looked like one. He was strong and could bend just about anything. But more important than his strength, was his ability to persuade.

He knew cars and *understood* them. Any woman knows on sight that cars are obstinate and male. Men get along with cars. Women get towed.

In chancy situations, Tom Keeper was calm. His face was stoic. He moved his glance to what was happening, but he didn't have tunnel vision and ignore everything else. He kept the whole area under his observation without seeming to do so.

Just like his daddy.

Tom was a man in the sense we all suppose males are. He never took a hand, in anything, unless he was needed. Then he was logical. Or he was physical, if it came to that. He caught arms, stopped fists with his open hand, or just said, "Be quiet" like you would to a dog or a child or an adult male who wasn't really in control of himself.

Women tended to go to Tom when they had problems with another man. Like Kayla Fuller had when she'd been baffled on how to regain her stupid ex-husband Tyler.

And it was Tom who took over the dogs from Kayla when she bought them at an illegal dog pit and didn't know what to do with them.

The fact that Kayla had never been interested in anyone else but that budding lawyer, Tyler, was obvious to everyone but Tom. He had really thought he had another chance with Kayla.

During that time Tom had been with Kayla he'd listened to her. And after a while he'd mentioned to her that she still loved Tyler. The woman had been shocked and strongly denied it, but Tom had watched Kayla as she'd protested that she was finished with Tyler. She'd protested too emotionally. She'd cried.

It had been a sad time for Tom. He'd still felt the same way about Kayla as he had before Tyler had intruded onto the scene. Tom had always thought that when he wanted to settle down, Kayla would be available.

But she'd loved Tyler. That had been a stunning observation. A nasty realization. How could she?

Her marriage to Tyler had been a waste of a good woman. At best, Tom thought, women were a trial. It made Tom wonder why God had given men such odd companions. Such baffling, complicated solutions to a man's needs. Women were a chore for any needy man. Women wanted men to do so much *else!*

The men from the distant past were probably the smartest. They protected the village, hunted and supplied the meat while the women kept the village neat and did the planting.

Theirs was a better organization. Their women had other women to ease them and listen to them. Women understood other women. Men never really did.

But at the current time, in TEXAS, with the women being snatched up by other men, Tom felt like an abandoned coyote outside the corral. How was Tom to get his sheep? How was he to live like everybody else, here, on this land? He was of the age when he needed to be paired off and responsible.

Why was his family named Keeper? What had somebody, back long ago, been keeper...of? Did the long ago Keepers raid other places and not give anything back?

Tom's eyes narrowed and he thought how he'd like to raid Tyler's house, snatch Kayla and keep—her. His ancestors very probably raided other places and stole women. His name wasn't keep-im or keep-it. It was keep-er.

Tom tilted his head and considered raiding. It was attractive to him. The urge was probably genetic. Since the Keepers had so much land and money, Tom finally wondered just how the devil they'd gotten all that land and all that money.

So the next time he saw his daddy, he asked him. They were out on the Keeper place, looking around, seeing what was going on. They'd come to a small stream with a large oak for shade.

The two were resting their horses. So they had stepped down and stood talking, letting the horses look around without the human weight on their backs.

There were three big dogs with them. The dogs were watching around and probably exchanging comments about where they were and what the humans were up to. The dogs were probably glad not to be horses. No saddles, no bridles, they went around almost free.

They listened as Tom asked his daddy, "How come we've got all this land and all this money?"

For the dogs it was not an interesting subject, so they went off a ways and looked around.

But Tom's father looked at his son and replied soberly and with a tad of puzzlement, "The reason we got this place is that we worked our tails off."

"How'd you go about getting the land?"

"I asked my daddy that same question when I was just a tad." He then commented in an aside, "It's interesting it took you so long to inquire about that." Then he looked afar as he instructed his twenty-eight-year-old son, "When our family wanted to come here, back then, just by the strangest chance, our ancestor learned the Indian chief of the tribe that lived on this land then could speak English. Your seven greats grandfather heard a conversation by the purest accident. The chief not only spoke English, he'd been to Europe!"

"Now why had he gone there?"

Tom's daddy said, "He was curious how come all us strange, pale people were invading their lands. He did sell us this plot and charged us a tad more than anybody else around here paid."

"Where'd the tribe go from here?"

And his daddy told him, "North to Canada. They didn't have the European rifles. Just their bows and arrows. They saw the future."

Tom considered as he looked around. Then he said, "It must have been tough for them to leave here."

"Apparently not. Other tribes were vicious in defending their land, but the small tribe we contacted was ready to leave here. They didn't much cotton to us newcomers and went off on their own to another place."

Tom said, "I've had it pretty easy."

His daddy agreed, "Just saying that shows you're getting ready to share the load. You're through school five years, now. You've traveled. That part's important. You got so's you realize how lucky we are to have this spread, and you understand you need to pull your share. About time you settled down."

Tom said sadly, "I thought I had the woman I wanted, but she went back to her husband."

His daddy nodded as he named them. "Kayla Davie went back to Tyler Fuller. Sometimes that happens. Women aren't at all predictable. She probably thinks she can help Tyler be a really great lawyer, and she could be right. But don't you fret none, you'll find a woman for yourself. Like I found your mama."

"How'd you find Mama?" Tom tilted his head back so that he could look at his daddy from under his Stetson brim.

His daddy gazed off across their land, remembering. "I'd really planned on being a bachelor. With seven brothers, I didn't think it was at all vital to the family that I get married and have kids. Then your mama came along on a horse that was limping..."

Tom waited. Then he responded, "I don't think I've heard this particular part of your life. What happened when Mama came up on a limping horse?"

"I was out looking for a heifer that was due, and she'd gone off into the bushes and got lost or killed or something. And your mama came along up on that limping horse." From under the oak, he looked at the horizon. Then he looked at the nearby nuisance, the lacy mesquite trees. He said softly, "She was really something."

Tom inquired, "She push a stone under the horse's shoe?"

"Now, I never even once thought of something like that happening! I just wonder if that could have been so!"

Tom licked his smiling lips and waited.

"She was so concerned about the horse. She asked if I'd look at it. That she was late getting back to the Sullivans'. I'd heard the Sullivans had company, and I'd been invited over for their dance that weekend. I let my unmarried brothers go. I stayed here. I had no need to meet some woman like that who was visiting."

"So she came looking for you?"

His father snorted. "Well, I never even *once*

thought of it thataway! Do you suppose she trapped me? She said she was just out riding. It was fretful to find her all by herself like that. I scolded her.''

"What'd she do." Not a question but just a nudge for his daddy to go on with the story.

"She told me to hush and fix her horse's foot. Think of a person calling a hoof a foot.''

And Tom remembered. "She wasn't a ranch girl.''

"Naw. City.''

"So what happened?''

"She flung a leg over the horse's neck and almost slid down. I caught her in time and pulled her away from the horse.''

Tom mused, "That horse would have been too old to be the one that was their biter.''

"It was a grandparent of that one that's such a nuisance.'' But his daddy was remembering. "Your mama was nice to hold. Women are just…different.''

"She let you *hold* her?''

"She wiggled and objected. She was so soft!''

"Daddy, you shock me. Now don't tell me your hands got out of control on her.''

"Heavens to Betsy, no! I was in shock or they might have! I couldn't think clear a-tall, boy. I was sundered right then.''

"What'd you do about the stone under the horse's shoe?''

"I put your mama aside very carefully and told her to stand still. Of course, she didn't do as I directed. But then, you know your mama. Nobody can direct her.''

"So you quarreled?''

"Oh, no. I went to the horse who was really

peeved. How ever that stone got under his shoe, it was a chore getting it out! I asked your mama-to-be how that stone had happened? She said that she'd gone through the creek.''

"That wasn't far from where you were, was it?''

"She never did admit to anything. She just watched me and waited. She didn't flirt or talk or anything. She surely was a beautiful young woman.'' He shook his head once. "She made me prickle.''

"So that was when she wrapped you around her little finger and just kept you thataway?''

"Yep. That about tells the whole story.''

"Did you get the stone out of the horse's shoe? Or did you just watch her?''

And his daddy said, "So you understand what a woman can do to a man? Was that Kayla rattling you?''

"Yeah.''

His daddy sighed with some regret. "I got to tell you she's really something. I agree to that. I just wonder why you didn't do your chasing before she met Tyler?''

Tom explained, "I didn't really notice.'' Tom was gently turning his head, looking around. "Then there was such a choice! I thought I had the time.''

"Men are greedy.''

"Yeah.''

There was a thoughtful silence. Then his dad advised, "You better get to looking farther for other women and get serious. Men snatch them up awful quick.''

"Do you suppose the magic She will come out here on a limping horse?''

"Who's that?"

"Mama did it for you. Think there's a woman who could cotton to me?"

His daddy frowned as he studied his son. Still frowning, he observed, "You got all the parts. You look good. You seem smart enough. I think you're a catch. You be careful you get a good woman. Don't get panicked and bring in a shrew."

"I'll try not to."

"Yeah." His daddy watched his son for a full minute. Then he sighed and mounted his horse. He asked, "Coming?"

Tom came out of his thoughtfulness and looked up at his father. "Hmmm?"

"What you thinking, boy?" His voice was gentle.

"I think I'll go over to the prairie dog kingdom and see how the dog is doing. He might be lonesome."

"Go by the house and take Queenie along."

Tom had been pensive. But as his daddy's words soaked in, he smiled a tad and he said, "Right."

Tom watched as his father moseyed off on his horse. The dogs chose to go with his dad.

Tom went to his own horse and took up the reins. He looked at the horse and indicated the bunch leaving them as he asked Oscar, "You that easy?"

The horse blew through his loose lips in disgust at such a question, then walked on off with his burden.

So at the ranch house yard, Tom whistled for Queenie. Think of a dog having such a name. It must irritate the hell out of her. They'd labeled her Queenie while Tom was gone, so he hadn't had any part of

the naming. But she was now used to being called
such a name.

It was rather apologetically that Tom called to
Queenie. She came with curiosity. That was the best
part of her. She was endlessly curious. If something
went into a hole, she watched, but she looked around
to see if there was an exit hole. She was an unusually
smart dog.

Tom told the other dogs to run along, but he took
Queenie. He closed the gate so that the other couple
of dogs stayed where they were supposed to be.

It didn't take forever to get out to where the prairie
dogs lived. The holes were many and the ground was
bare and hilly from their digging.

As soon as they approached the prairie dog mound,
the dog was there. It was the dog that Kayla Davie
Fuller had bought from the dogfight pit and one of
those given to Tom to find a home.

The dog was not a family dog or even a barn dog.
It was a loner. However, the dog did notice Queenie
quite avidly. He ignored the human and the horse and
was zeroed in on the female dog. She wagged her tail
and her smile was big.

Off a way, Tom stepped down from the saddle and
watched, not intruding. Queenie obviously communicated with the big, mended dog, who had fighting
scars and healed rips. She was impressed. The big dog
moved and watched her watch him. She continued her
pleased smile.

The two looked at the prairie dog hill. The dog in
charge apparently told her why he was there. That he
was invaluable in keeping the rodents under some
control.

She apparently was curious. So after several serious tries, he caught her a prairie dog and gave it to her, laying it before her.

Queenie was intently curious. She sniffed the gift, and it flipped over to run! The male caught it again! It wasn't dead! He'd given Queenie a live one.

Tom watched, absolutely fascinated. How amazing to realize what the male dog was doing to impress the female. How typical of all males to show off, and willingly be the slave of a female. After she'd eaten the little creature, the dog took Queenie to a small rill that emptied into a bigger stream down a ways.

She lapped the water. She looked at the male dog and then lapped some more. She had indicated to her host that the water was good.

There was no difference between the males of all species. The male courted the female in the very similar ways of all males. They all communicated.

After a time, Tom went to his horse, mounted and turned it slowly to go back to the ranch house. He went diagonally, at first, so that he could look back at the dogs.

Queenie saw that he was leaving. She watched but since he did not call to her, she didn't feel committed to follow. She turned alertly to the male dog and her smile was big.

The male dog stood with his head up and his neck stretched, watching after the human on the horse. Then he turned and looked at the bitch. He smiled. She moved and flirted and played around the big dog.

He sat and laughed.

Tom left knowing that delivering Queenie to the isolated dog had been a good thing. The fact that he'd supplied another male with a handy, willing female was balm to his own lonely feelings. Tom had helped a male to a life of better interest. And apparently Queenie hadn't minded at all.

Then Tom wondered who in the world had named that female dog…Queenie? When the two dogs met just what real name had she'd given as hers to the male and what real name had the male supplied as his?

For some reason, Tom turned his horse away from the direction of the ranch and toward the stream. There he allowed his horse to drink rather slowly and quite a bit. He encouraged it as he went upstream and also drank water. The man and his horse were oddly silent and watchful.

The horse kept looking up and to a certain spot. He blew his lips as he watched and lifted his head higher.

Tom glanced around the area and was aware they were very alone. Then he noticed the attention of the horse, and he looked out and away. He saw nothing to cause the horse to give such attention.

Then Tom saw a dot in the distance that was a dog. With a deep breath and using his fingers in his mouth, he whistled the ranch double whistle for dogs at that distance, and the dog came his way. Tom noticed it had come from some distance, and that it was not one of the ranch dogs. It was the human whistle that caught the dog's attention. It walked oddly.

Tom told the horse, "Steady."

Although it wasn't yet summer, the dog could have rabies. Sick dogs generally left home. Or he could be lost. And he could be a calf killer. The approaching creature could be just about anything.

The man and the horse looked other places, to keep track of the area, but they were for the most part concentrated on the approaching dog.

Because of the waterless area beyond, Tom didn't go to meet the dog. If it had come across that stretch of barren land, it would be thirsty, and there was water close to where Tom was standing.

The dog could smell it. He was urgent to turn back, but the water lured him on. And Tom remembered that he and the horse had drunk especially—for a reason. Was there a person out there on the flat, alone? In danger? Harmed? Where would he be? She?

With more intentness, Tom watched the approaching dog. So did the horse. The dog was coming from a bleak area. The land was used to graze cattle—on occasion—depending on how the weather had been, which year. If it'd been wet, there'd be enough growth for a herd, if it had been dry, other places were used. Beyond, the land was fragile.

When the dog came to the water, it was still some distance from where Tom stood. It walked into the water and lapped carefully.

To gulp water immediately could flounder a creature. The dog was dehydrated. The dog looked at Tom but did not attempt to approach him. It was mostly trying to adjust to the water. And it began to shiver.

The water was too cool for the dog.

Concerned, Tom carefully went toward the dog. It didn't try to get away. It watched, shivering. But it wouldn't get out of the water. It lapped some and shivered.

It tried to bark, to communicate, but its throat was raw from the lack of water and a long journey.

Tom took out his cellular phone and called in to the house. "This is Tom."

"It's Joe," came the answer. "What's up?"

"An exhausted, dehydrated dog just came in off the upper flats. He's in the stream but he isn't yet drinking much."

"Is anybody following him?"

Tom looked around again out to the edge of forever. "Not that I can see."

"I'll bring some of the boys out and a couple of tracers," Joe suggested. "If he's available, it might help if Rip goes up in the plane and looks around. We'll have him land out by you so he can find the dog's tracks. Keep in touch. If the dog should leave, go along but let us know."

"Right."

"We'll be along as soon as possible." That had a meaning of immediate commitment.

And quite sure there was need, Tom said, "Thank you."

The answering reply was a serious, "Yeah."

Slowly, Tom began to move toward where the dog was. If the dog stayed put, he was probably used to people. But Tom knew he'd never get the dog to stay close. It wasn't looking for a place but for help.

How strange that Tom felt that so clearly.

He watched the dog and told it, "You need to get out of that water and shake yourself dry so's you won't chill."

The dog shivered.

Tom unsaddled his horse and took the blanket off.

"Come here, boy. I'll help you. You chill, you'll get really sick. Who've you left out there? Where are they?"

The dog lapped several times. Then he went to the edge of the water in the shallows and shook himself hard, sending water flying everywhere. It was as if he'd understood Tom's words.

Tom said, "Let me just put this blanket on you."

The dog became careful. He watched but he was not at all sure the man should come closer.

Tom backed away and put the blanket aside.

Tom took note of the slight indentations of the dog's arriving paw marks. How far across the plain could the prints be followed? How far had that dog come?

Would the dog have come to the stream directly? Or would he have circled, looking for a habitation? Looking for people.

Tom listened for the plane.

A plane would cover the area much quicker. If the dog was that dehydrated, so would be whoever the dog had left out there, on the tableland.

One

Rip Morris landed the range plane near Tom Keeper with casual finesse. He was a casual man, lazy-eyed and aloof. He was also one hell of a pilot. He had eyes like a hawk. He could spot anything...even if it couldn't move.

As Tom went over to the two-seater, exposed-cockpit plane, Rip was throttling it down. He pushed up his goggles and lifted the flaps on his helmet. He needed a shave. That wasn't unusual.

Tom tersely said, "I think there's a person out there that this dog is worried about. How about you taking the dog up and go slow enough that the dog just might know where you are and where he's been?"

And Rip regarded the medium-sized dog, who was mostly black with some white, with a measured look.

Get the damned dog aloft, Rip thought, and it would probably throw up, or see something and jump out. No sweat. It was the dog's funeral.

So with some effort and no help from Rip at all, Tom got the dog in the front cockpit. Tom suggested, "You might just go along low and slow and see how the dog reacts."

Rip nodded once as he said, "Wait here." He revved the engine and took off.

Rip flew the plane low and slow, allowing him to follow the dog's trail on the ground. The trail did circle, but the plane was by then up high enough that Rip could see farther.

Remarkably, the dog didn't try to jump out, but its attention was riveted. Then, from the back cockpit, Rip noticed that the dog wasn't looking along the way, its attention was ahead. They went quite a way, even flying. Then the dog's head moved in little adjustments.

Way ahead, there was a tiny spiral of buzzards.

The dog barked.

It turned and barked again at Rip. But under the distant spiral of waiting buzzards, Rip had already seen the speck-sized, floundered horse with a person trapped underneath it. Rip throttled down and did a low, slow circle. The buzzards rose higher, and Rip had the room he needed to land.

The horse did not move. The trapped person raised a feeble hand. Well, hell. Whoever it was under that horse was still alive but probably damn near dead.

But the dog was smart enough not to jump out yet. He squeak-barked down at the still horse and the raised arm—and he stayed in the plane. But he squeak-barked back at Rip as if to tell him to land.

Rip gave the dog an enduring glance. He then turned the plane, easing it down slowly in a wide circle so as not to stir up too much dust in the low grasses.

As he turned, Rip called in to the ranch, telling exactly where he was and to call Tom Keeper. He was told he needed to release the guy from under the horse without hurting him worse. Rip said he'd see if he could do that while he waited for the other planes to get there. Yeah, he had extra water.

Rip's disgruntled mind wondered why the hell that guy was out there in that empty area with only a horse and a dog. People are stupid. It only takes one stupid nut to tie up the whole area looking for him. Rip remembered that was how Jones had crashed, looking for some dumb pilgrim who didn't know enough to pay attention to where he was. At that time, the storm was such that the flooding land pockets on the plain could drown a man.

After saving the damned pilgrim, Jones's spirit had probably just trudged on off to heaven feeling he'd done his share. He would've had no hostility about stupidity like Rip Morris was grinding his teeth over, right then, for another pilgrim out—alone on a plain—and trapped under a dead horse.

If he'd had somebody with him, he wouldn't have been this bad. On top of all that, he had invaded private land without permission.

With skill, Rip landed the plane downwind so that no dirt blew over the motionless horse or the man.

The dog was out of the cockpit first. It went to the man, sniffed and looked up at Rip urgently.

Rip got the water bag and went carefully to the man who was trying to speak. His tongue was swollen. His leg was trapped under the dead horse.

Rip took out a clean handkerchief and soaked it to lay it on the man's mouth. Then he dribbled water onto it as he talked, soothing, telling the man that others would be there shortly.

And they were. Planes landed downwind. They avoided the buzzards and did as Rip had done. The men came with ropes and pulled the dead horse away with care. They talked to the man who was, by then, covered with blankets so that he wouldn't chill further.

The injured, dehydrated man was put on a stretcher, carried to the cargo plane and put inside. The dog tried to get into the plane, but Rip held him.

The dog hoarsely tried to bark, not fighting or growling but lunging in Rip's firm grip. It just showed that Rip knew animals. He talked gently the entire time, soothing, explaining.

Watching the rescue plane rising from the ground, the dog shivered and sat still. Rip tied a blanket around the dog. Then he carried the dog back to his own plane, leaving others to find where the horse had been, who the man could be and why the hell he'd been out there alone.

Rip got into the plane and flew back to the ranch. On the plane's communication radio, he told Joe what all had taken place. Then he told about the dog. He was coming in with the dog. Rip asked Joe, "Could you see if one of the vets is available?"

So when Rip landed, there was an interesting number of people available. The dog shivered. They took the dog and put him on a stretcher and, still wrapped in the blanket, they carried him into the vet's bailiwick.

People can be very kind to humans who are in distress, but they are doubly so with animals. Animals aren't as informed nor is there the communication between the human and the animal.

In his house, Rip slept next to the dog that night. He wakened every couple of hours to give the dog water and made sure the dog was all right. This man was a loner. He had no real use for the rest of the population.

Well, he had gone out to help find a lost person more than that one time. But he never had much compassion for any of them. They'd been stupid. If they'd paid attention to just the basics of logical thinking, they would have never gotten in the binds in which they'd managed to trap themselves.

Rip called the hospital the next morning and said, "Tell what's his name, that the Keepers' crew found out on the plain, that his dog's doing fine."

And the snippy nurse asked, "Is this Rip Morris?"

"Yeah."

"The person's name is Andrew Parsons. He is doing as well as can be expected. He's still rather fragile right now—"

"Just tell 'im his dog's okay."

"—and his sister's here. She's really grateful to you for finding him. She wants to thank you."

"Tell her she's welcome to the damned fool. The

dog is smarter and worth more than the dumb nut you've got to save."

The nurse sassed, "You tend to be somewhat prejudiced and opinionated."

"Knowing that, saves you."

And the snippy nurse said in a very prissy manner, "If we could get through the quagmire of lurid magazines and reach what is left of the core of your altered brain, we might make some headway in civilizing you."

"I don't read something as mild as that."

"You need help."

"Naw. Tell the pilgrim his dog's okay. That'll give him something to think about. Don't mention the horse is dead as yet. He killed it, taking it out there. It looked like a good horse, too. The dumb bastard."

And the snippy nurse retorted, "You need therapy."

"What kind?"

"Not what you're thinking." And she hung up.

That didn't bother Rip one bit. He was used to women hanging up on him...after they'd called him all sweet and honey. But he didn't want a female who was all sweetness and honey. He wanted a woman. He wanted a woman who was different from what he'd known. He wanted a partner.

He hated gigglers. He hated tart and snippy women. Why couldn't women be more like men? Not that he could be lured by any man. He just wanted a female who had the logic and straightforwardness of the male thinking. A woman who could handle a surprise mouse without shrieking and carrying on from the top of the table. Was that asking too much?

Rip simply could not tolerate a vapid woman whose mind was lost in materials and colors and clever food bits. A woman like that, irritated him.

So it was about three days later, and he still hadn't shaved. Rip had an okay from the vet, so he took the dog to the humans' hospital. He did that so the man, Andrew Parsons, might understand the dog was okay. However, it was mostly so that the anxious dog could see the man. A fly head, like that man, was a heavy responsibility for any dog.

Rip took a silent, patient breath when he realized the stupid nurse was there. But then she said, "His sister would like to see you."

Hell.

He'd thought, at that time of the morning, visitors wouldn't be underfoot. It was for the *dog* that he was there. The dog was superior. But he was restless and anxious.

Why on earth had the dog gotten tangled up with an owner who was so stupid? Poor dog. Just maybe, the man would allow Rip to take the dog off his hands. If not permanently, at least getting away for a while from the pilgrim would be a respite for the dog.

There was the snippy nurse saying, "—and this is Rip Morris" to a woman who had just approached them.

Rip looked at the pilgrim's sister with naked eyes of shock. The sun-squint lines beside his eyes disappeared and there were the white lines that had been hidden by the sun squint. His lips parted, and he looked vulnerable. He was.

Rip had not heard her name.

The woman held out her hand and her handshake was a good firm one that didn't tickle or rub or flirt. Her hand was small but her grip was just right. So were her eyes.

The irises were blue and she wore a hell of a lot of mascara or she'd had those false eyelashes planted. If she blinked the wind from those lashes might knock him back a step. He said, "How do you do." No question. She needn't reply.

Then he realized she wasn't interested in him. Thank God for that. Women tended to be pushy.

She was saying, "—first there. Thank you."

He nodded. She wasn't moving her body to call attention to herself. She was just talking about her brother.

Because it had baffled them all, Rip asked the sister, "Why was he out there?"

"I haven't heard." That's what she replied. She did not expand on it. She wasn't particularly interested in visiting. She just wanted to thank the first person there who had helped her stupid brother.

Of course, she didn't call her brother stupid. That was only Rip's I.D. for him. Rip asked again, "Why the *hell* was he out there all alone, on that plain? The grass was too low even for grazing. Who the hell would be out that way if he got in trouble?"

"You were."

"That's *only* because the dog came limping in, and Tom Keeper called me."

And she said in a level manner, "Oh. Then it's Tom Keeper whom I must thank."

Somehow that stuck in Rip's craw. "I'll pass the word along."

"How nice."

Rip frowned at her. Snippy. Who cared what she was? Not him. He took the dog over to the hospital bed and told the nurse, "He's had a bath and been defleaed."

She grinned.

Now *that's* how women were supposed to react. But his face didn't smile nor did he look at the nurse. He looked at the man on the bed. Andrew Parsons. He looked like a parson from olden times. Probably was a descendant of one. He told the silent man, "Your dog is here to see to you. Open your eyes and look at him so's he'll know you're okay."

The nurse protested, "He's drug—"

But with some effort, Andrew opened his eyes and his head turned very, very slowly. The dog put his paws on the side of the bed and he made an anxious throat sound.

Andrew's hand came slowly, slowly up and sideways until it touched the dog's neck.

The dog licked Andrew's hand, the nurse gasped and reached, but Rip's hands stopped her and he wouldn't let her go.

She was furious, but she looked up at Rip who was simply watching the dog. So she did also, and the dog licked the man's hand again.

Rip murmured to the nurse, "Good, clean dog spit."

She shuddered.

But there was the slightest smile on Andrew's face. His eyes closed. There was a long exhale of breath and his body seemed to dissolve. There were several gasps there in the room. All female.

Rip looked at the sister. She was watching her brother intently. The nurse took Andrew's wrist and felt the heartbeat. She'd thought he'd died. His breathing was so slow. But it was steady. He had sunk down into deep sleep.

The dog looked at Rip. He told the dog, "He's okay. You can stay fifteen minutes, then we'll go home and you can come back this afternoon."

Rip was actually letting the nurse know how he was going to let the dog come visit. She took a protesting breath, but the floor doctor was at the door.

The doctor came inside the room and took up Andrew's wrist. The doctor didn't push the dog aside but left him with his forefeet on the side of the bed.

The doctor lifted one of Andrew's eyelids and listened to his breaths, then he said, "He's sleeping very nicely. He needs to sleep. This has been a very tough time." Then he turned to Rip and smiled. And he said, "Thank you for bringing his dog up. Do it again this afternoon. Andrew has been restless and frowning. Obviously, he's been worried about the dog. Knowing the dog is all right, Andrew will rest better."

"When's the best time?" That was Rip's response to the obvious logic.

"We'll stimulate him and shift him. We'll wake him about two. Come then."

"Okay."

"—and bring the dog."

"Of course."

As Rip left the room with the dog, the patient's sister followed. She had not protested the dog or the man, and it was now that she said, "Thank you for bringing Buddy along."

"So that's his name?" Rip found himself looking at the snippy woman. She was a looker without doing anything about it. She didn't have on any makeup other than those eyelashes and her hair was casual.

She said, "Andrew and Buddy are good friends... buddies."

"That's why the dog went looking for help."

"Is that how you found him?"

"The son of our boss, Tom Keeper, saw the dog first. He sent out the alarm. He was on horseback. I had a plane. I took Buddy and flew low and we found him...Andrew." And again Rip asked, "What the *hell* was Andrew doing out in that territory?"

"I have no idea."

About then, the doctor came up the corridor and smiled as he said, "There's a boy who should see Buddy. Would you mind taking a little more time?"

Being a loner, visiting wasn't one of the things Rip chose to do. But how could he refuse when he knew the dog was a curious creature? Actually, the dog was nosy. So Rip said to the doctor, "Lead the way."

The thing that surprised Rip most was that the sister...whose name he hadn't heard...was following. She must be bored just sitting next to her sleeping brother. But then, what good would that do, just sitting by a man who was entirely out of it?

So what's-her-name went along. She had a good, easy walk.

The doctor told Rip, "There's a very lonely boy whose home is a long way from here. He has brothers and sisters who call him, but he doesn't have any visitors. He, too, has a bad leg. But his is broken.''

The boy's name was Chuck. He lay in bed with his leg elevated somewhat by a complicated bunch of wires. He was pale and very quiet. He was watching TV.

In an aside, the doctor said to Rip, "Thank God for TV children's shows.''

Two nurses said softly, "Amen.''

Andrew's sister asked, "But do the kids get together and watch?''

The doctor nodded. "Those who can walk. Some of them come here, if they're not too ill.''

The doctor went in the boy's room. "Hello, Chuck. May I bring in a friend?''

The boy turned his head slowly. "Yeah.''

And the dog came in alertly, looking. Did he expect to see Andrew again? He put his feet up against the high bed and looked at the patient.

The boy was delighted! "Hello!" he exclaimed. "How'd you get inside?''

And the doctor said, "His master is in the hospital. He's asleep. The dog's name is Buddy. I thought you might like to know him.''

Chuck smiled and put out his hand. The dog, Buddy, gave the boy's hand a lick, and Chuck smiled as he petted the dog.

It was a nice thing to watch. But the doctor had to leave and did so quietly.

The nurse said to Chuck, "Don't put your hand on your face or in your mouth until I've washed it.''

They all laughed, but the important laugh was Chuck's.

* * *

After fifteen minutes, the nurse in charge reluctantly signaled Rip to leave. Rip told Chuck, "We'll see you this afternoon."

Another visit from the dog was something for the boy to anticipate.

The nurses were charming in their goodbyes.

Andrew's sister watched those people leave before she said to Rip, "Thank you for coming. Andrew will be so glad to see Buddy again this afternoon. I know keeping the dog and bringing him here takes your time. Is Buddy a problem for you?"

"Naw. He just goes along with me. He likes flying."

She actually looked *at* him as she asked, "What sort of flying do you do?"

He returned her look, and he found he liked the way she watched him. He told her, "I look at crops, at the height of grasses, for vans that are off the highway and could be rustlers after cattle...and I look for people who don't have cellular phones and can be lost."

She watched him soberly. "...or trapped under a dead horse."

"I mostly look for our guys. Andrew is my first foreigner." Well, he wasn't from another land, so Rip added, "A nonresident...trespasser." His tongue just added that. It was true. Andrew hadn't had permission to trod on acreage that was private land.

Andrew's sister guessed, "He was where he wasn't supposed to be?"

"Exactly." Then without his permission, Rip's tongue just went on, "He could have gone to any highway rest stop and inquired as to how he might go anywhere. There are state cops at almost all the rest stops. They give information. Nobody intrudes on private lands. And to go over a fence and out on the lands and get lost is a great nuisance for the owners and crews on the places. It takes our time and concern. We are busy people.''

"How are you managing?" She gestured. Then, realizing that wasn't enough, she added, "Coming here and taking care of Buddy?"

Rip looked at Andrew's sister and thought it was probably a good thing he didn't know her name. She lured him. He didn't want that kind of serious, unknowing lure. He sighed and said, "I manage. He's a good dog. My boss gives me the time to bring him to see the pilgrim." He almost instantly bit his lip.

"Pilgrim?"

It was not a kind name. Rip had used it to mean a person who'd landed where nobody wanted him. So Rip said, "Uhhh. Well, he was new to us."

Andrew's sister nodded. Then she said, "If anything…changes…I could call you and save you the time coming into town. Is there a phone number where I can reach you?"

He asked, "What's your name?"

"Lu."

Thoughtfully tilting his head back, Rip questioned, "Wasn't there a song about a lady named Lu?"

"Probably. My dad named me. He's a…different person. He baffles my mother."

Without any warning, Rip found himself blurting, "I never knew my parents." His teeth went back into his lower lip. They should have stayed there.

Lu guessed. "You left home as soon as you could."

"Yeah." They'd left him. He watched her a minute with his eyes slitted. He'd never given his phone number to any woman. "Don't you give my number to anybody, do you hear me?"

She began to smile. "Women throw themselves in front of your car?"

"Any man gets tired of being hounded."

"Hounded." She tasted the word. Then she inquired with the slightest smile, "You're implying women are...hounds?"

Rip slowly shook his head, as he said very seriously, "Not all of them. Some really good women live in this world."

She was curious about his replies so she asked, "But there are...females who...hound you?"

Rip shrugged logically. "—and there're the male variety of—hounds," he admitted. "I'm one every now and again." He watched her. He became aware that she was tired and had been concerned and worried about that stupid brother of hers. "You got a place here to stay that's convenient?"

"Yes. Just down the block, there's a hospice. This hospital services a large area."

"Yeah. People like Chuck who come a long way."

"He's a nice little boy. I met his mother."

"How'd you do that?"

"I can't just sit in Andrew's room. So these last few days, I've helped out...distributed books, that sort of thing."

Rip didn't verbally praise her but his smile was a benediction. He gave her his phone number. Just doing that, wobbled him. He told her, "Remember, you don't give that to *any*body, do you hear me?"

Very seriously she replied, "I'll have a blind tattooer put it on my body in a discreet place."

Rip groused, "And you'll tell him what to tattoo. He'll know the number."

She licked her smile. "I'll do the tattooing. He won't have a clue."

Rip tilted his head back and squinted his eyes. "Where you gonna put my number?"

"No one will ever know."

"Remember to burn the paper."

"Of course."

Again Rip squinted his eyes at her and asked softly, "How you gonna see the number if you're in public?"

She considered. "Be sure the telephone booth door is closed?"

"That's when the light goes on. When the door's closed." He watched her more closely.

"I'll find a private phone, if it's important to call you."

"Oh." He studied her with a serious face. "I thought you just meant that you'd want to talk to me."

"No," she reminded him. "The phone number is because I might need to cancel you coming here if Andrew is out of it or something like that."

"Well." He hesitated and looked around rather stubbornly. "I thought you were interested in... uh...the boy."

"Chuck."

"Yeah. Him. Don't you think it's important for

Buddy to come visit the kid? Even if your brother's out, the kid might like to see Buddy.''

She considered that quite seriously and finally nodded just a tad. "You could be right."

"So we'll see you this afternoon. Uh. You wanna go out for lunch?"

"With the dog?"

"We can go to a drive-in."

"I don't think I can even look at another hamburger."

"There're drive-ins that have Mexican food."

"Anything else?"

"Soup?"

"My stomach might accept soup."

He considered her with a still face. He understood that she loved her brother. Her stomach was scared over him and she was having trouble eating. He'd take her to Marge's. She'd get the soup.

Well, Marge was in a tizzy with Rip's phone call. Rip was bringing a woman to her stand for soup! He was bringing along a woman! For Pete's sakes alive, who'd ever believe that Rip would bring a woman out at *noon!* What the *hell* was happening?

And there he came in his pickup. He had a dog with him and a woman. She was there! A woman in broad daylight! And she looked like a normal woman. No exotic makeup, all smeared. Her clothes were simple and rather blah. What was happening to Rip!

The woman was kin? She was someone else's wife? He was responsible for some guy's wife? Or lover? The woman didn't look like a lover. She looked more like she'd been pulled through a knot-hole. She looked tired and quite pale.

So Marge figured they'd been in bed together for at least a day or two. It made Marge a little jealous. She called out to her husband, Hank. He needed to see what could happen between couples.

Marge said to the pale woman when she and Rip walked in, "I'm Marge. This here's my husband, Hank."

The pale woman said, "How do you do?"

She was a lady. Marge knew that right away, but what in the world was Rip doing with a lady, for Pete's sake? If he stayed around something like her for very long he'd be ruined!

Rip told Hank, who was the real cook in the place, "How about some kind of gentle soup for her?" Then wanting to make an impression on Lu, he added kindly, "She's been through a lot these last several days."

Marge knew it! The two had been holed up in Rip's bed all that while and the woman was starving! It was no *wonder* that she looked so tired.

Marge looked over at Rip with a serious frown for such a greedy man, but her wrinkled face smoothed out and she smiled just a little. No woman would complain, even after being in bed with Rip for three days running. Three days of being moved around on a bed by him. Ahhh. He was really something.

Marge smiled at the woman and asked softly, "You okay?"

And the woman replied, "I'm fine."

Marge laughed. Any woman would've answered thata way.

But Marge's laughing response made Lu blink. What could be so amusing about having a brother in a hospital?

The soup came with crackers and there was a glass of milk. As anyone would, Rip had two hamburgers and a beer. On the side he asked for a double patty of raw meat with milk.

Hank was forced to inquire, "That raw meat help?"

Marge immediately knew Hank was aware the couple had spent three days in bed together, and—

Rip mentioned kindly, "The dog's in the truck. He needs food just like the rest of us."

Marge understood the dog had been neglected during that three-day bed marathon. She said to Rip, "Next time you two get together, bring the dog here, and we'll take care of him."

That left the couple blank-faced. Although male and female, their faces were very similar. While Rip's eyes squinted a little as he tried to understand Marge's offer, Lu just went back to her soup. She'd found West TEXANS were a little strange and there was no purpose in trying to sort them out and finding a way to understand them. She'd be back home in East TEXAS by then.

Two

Marge and Hank's fast-food place was in an old house in a neighborhood that had lost most of its residential status. Their yard had been altered into a driveway, along which were parking places for those who wanted to eat inside. They didn't dine; they ate. The downstairs rooms of the house were separated eating places. It was casual.

In one room at one of the small tables, Lu and Rip slowly ate their lunch. The dog, Buddy, was allowed out of the pickup and on the cooler back porch. The dog didn't need to be tied and obeyed orders to stay.

Rip looked at Lu. When had he ever really looked at a woman just to see her? He realized what she needed most was a nap. She was wrung-out. He did not want to take her to the hospice. He'd not be welcomed to go to her room and waken her.

He looked at his watch. If they drove out to his house at the Keeper place, they'd just about, right away, have to drive back to the hospital for the two o'clock visit.

He asked Marge, "You got a bed for her to nap?"

Marge's eyes widened. He was going to get her out of his reach and let her rest! She asked carefully, "Just her?" In spite of her riveted interest, this was her own place and she couldn't really allow anything, well, anything like that in her place.

Rip replied, "I'm not as tired as her." In his manner of speech, the "tired" sounded like tarred.

But his comment made the misguided Marge burst into a quickly attempted smothered laugh. Obviously, his lust had outlasted Lu's. The exhausted, overly used, budding woman needed some rest, but she had to be out of his greedy reach!

So with her eyes flickering with suppressed interest, Marge said, "We got a bed upstairs."

Rip didn't like leaving Lu in a strange place alone, and while he'd gladly stay and protect her himself, he had her reputation to consider. So he asked, "Could Buddy stay with her? He's house-trained."

The dog was a problem, but Marge found the whole situation so fascinating, that she was ready to tolerate the dog. She said a rather hesitant but oddly quick, "Okay."

Then they had to convince Lu. She said, "No, I can't give you more to do. You're busy enough. I'll just go to the hospice."

"No." That, of course, was Rip. He tended to control.

Marge's eyes danced but her mouth was still and

did not smile. She said, "No problem. Really. You're welcome."

Just the idea of a bed, right then and there, had Lu saying, "You're very kind."

Marge, thinking on her own track, had figured erroneously why the young woman was so tired. Lu'd be given an hour or so of being left alone, by Rip, this time, and sleeping. Marge said, "Stay here for a while."

Very seriously, Rip agreed, as he said to Lu, "You can sleep."

Rip's and Marge's urging rather amused Lu, then, because she had just realized the clientele of the eatery would be noisy and laughing and banging dishes around. She said, "I could go back to the hospice."

"No, no." That time the response was almost in chorus with Rip, Marge and Hank all seriously protesting.

So it was Marge who led the draggingly tired young woman up the stairs, and Buddy went along without any human indication that he should go with her.

In the small room, the screened window was open to the spring air. The bed was big and soft.

The dog looked around and settled down under the window. He watched with his chin on his front paws.

Marge watched as Lu slid her dress off over her head. The young woman was obviously very weary. She crawled slowly onto the bed and pulled the light blanket up over her. She said to Marge, "This is like a cloud."

It was only then that Marge understood Lu wasn't only a love partner, she was also a young, tired human. Having never had children of her own, Marge awkwardly tugged on the blanket, setting it askew. Awkwardly, she said, ''Sleep tight, honey.''

Then Marge turned and went out the door, closing it gently.

So with the woman gone, the dog came over and jumped up on the bottom of the bed and curled around several times before it sighed and settled down.

That almost overly amused the tired Lu. She moved her feet over to one side, already cramped by the area the dog had taken as its own, but she did go right to sleep.

It was later that Lu felt the dog get up and cross over her covered, cramped legs to jump down onto the floor. His toenails clicked as he went over to the window to sit there. She opened her eyes to watch the dog. He was watching the door.

There was a soft knock and before she could say or do anything, the door opened. It was Rip. ''You awake?''

She said, ''The dog sleeps on the bed. He's a sham.''

''I didn't think he'd pull that on a fragile lady! I *am* shocked.'' He shook his head and tsked, looking at the dog.

Then with his lack of any surprise, she mentioned, ''Apparently, not very much.''

''I've gotten used to it in this time he's been with me. The curious part is he has no qualms about sleeping with somebody, but he's careful to be on the floor if somebody else comes along.''

She nodded. ''A total fraud.''

Rip asked gently, "Did you sleep at all?"

"Like a dead rock!"

"There are *live* rocks?" he gasped.

She groaned. "You're one of those kind who is easily shocked."

So, of course, he then said, "So you slept like a dead rock."

"I breathed."

With her words, Rip remembered their watching to be sure her brother in the hospital breathed. Her brother. Rip asked, "Where are your parents?"

"My daddy had a heart attack when he heard Andrew was missing. Mother's with him."

"Ahhhh. He okay?"

"It was mild. It might not have been a heart attack, as such as it was panic. He tends to be emotional. Our doctor is careful of him. My daddy talks to the medical staff here. They give him updates."

Rip by then had slowly moved to the side of her bed. He sat on the edge very carefully, like an animal who isn't sure of his welcome.

She asked logically, "How am I to get up and get dressed with you here?"

"I'll help."

"No. I'm capable. Go downstairs, and I'll be there in just a couple of minutes."

"You're selfish!" He made the two growling, hushed words into shock.

She considered for a minute and then nodded as she agreed, "Yep."

He looked disgruntled. He did a good job of it, but she wasn't lured. She was worse. She was patient.

Rip sighed with great drama, then he said to the

dog, "Come along, Buddy. If I can't stay here and watch her dress, then neither can you. You've already *slept* with her. I am surprised at you. Shame on you!"

The dog lifted his head, closed his eyes and panted oddly as if he was laughing.

She said, "It's as if—"

"Yeah. He thinks I'm funny. He laughs most of the time. And he tries to communicate. He thinks I'm real dumb."

She agreed with his study. "Dogs tend to be tolerant, but you wonder what sort of words they mumble under their breaths."

He nodded as he replied, "You've been the servant of dogs."

She shared: "Cats are less demanding. They can get up on tables easier than dogs. On beds, they at first pretend to be little, fluffy balls that take up no room at all. Then when you're asleep, they take the middle of the bed and sprawl out…sideways."

"Dogs are similar. They're surprised when any human objects to not having their share of the bed."

"How do you handle that?"

"I pitch the dog outside."

"In this weather?"

"It's spring for crying out loud! He ought to just sleep outside. He would, but there isn't a fence around my place."

"What sort of…place…do you have?"

"I fly for the Keeper ranch. My place is a shack in the quarter of the ranch where the peons work."

She guessed, "It probably just needs paint."

"Wanna help paint it?" He blinked at his mouth's

invitation but it didn't withdraw the question. He waited for her reply.

She watched him a minute with such a slight unknowing smile. Then she said, "I just might."

"Our boss and his sons are really busy with the ranch. They don't get much chance to do repairs out where I am."

She'd already met the Keepers. They'd been to the hospital early to be sure everything was okay. Tom Keeper had been especially kind. She smiled a tad.

Rip thought she was friendly. He asked, "You need a kiss to get you revved up and going?" Even that startled Rip. When had he ever had to ask for one?

Still smiling, she watched him for a minute then she barely shook her head.

"You probably got a fever. I'll just kiss your forehead and see."

So he did that. He was slow and careful. His breathing was obvious. He said, "You're hotter than a two-dollar pistol."

She denied that. "I'm as cool as the spring breeze."

"Any spring breeze is warm and friendly."

"Not this one."

"You need warming?"

She didn't dare reply to that one. She shook her head in a tremor and pulled the blanket up to her eyes.

He said, "Well, if you're that healthy, we gotta get going to be over there in time to see both Andrew and Chuck. Up and at 'em, you lazy woman."

Marge came and opened the door a little wider. She asked avidly, "You all going back to bed?"

"No. He's being rude and making me get up."

Marge smiled. "He's already up."

That went on by Lu, and she said, "Take him out of here so's I can dress."

That startled Marge. Why would the girl be so modest now? Luring. Maybe that was the trick. So she took hold of Rip's sleeve and said, "Come on, give her some privacy for a change."

That went over Rip's head. He said, "Who all's been crowding her?"

"Nobody here." Marge told Rip. "Come on, let her get her clothes on."

"Doesn't she have on *anything?*" He looked back.

But Marge pulled him through the door and closed it after them.

Out in the hall on the other side of the door, Rip objected, "The dog's still in there. He ought not get to look when you've dragged me out here, and left her in there with that nosy dog!"

Marge said snippily, "Not in my house, you don't." She was still positive the two had been together all those days and that was why Lu was so tired.

It was only then that Marge said with some astonishment, "Now, I know what's so different about you, you've *shaved!*" She gasped in amazement. She said, "You look good!" She acted just exactly like it was a surprise that he cleaned up so well.

That made Rip a little indignant. "I've shaved before this."

With some interest, Marge declared, "I don't recall ever seeing you with a naked face before now."

"You're just like every other woman I've run into." And being a gentleman, he moved Marge aside and went down the stairs ahead of her as his grand-maw had taught him. That was so's if a woman slipped, she'd run into him and not go all the way down the stairs, bumping on each and every step. Doing anything, like that, bruised a woman's bottom for some time. He was finalizing his protest to Marge, "You just don't notice me enough."

Behind him, Marge laughed all the rest of the way down the stairs.

When Lu finally came down the stairs, she was accompanied by the dog. Buddy walked alongside the female as if he was guarding her. He did that so's he wouldn't be pitched outside and left alone, unable to listen to the gossip or see whatever went on inside. So he was courteous and careful...and quiet.

Dogs are sly.

But he didn't fool Lu anymore. He had probably learned to hog the bed that way from some damned cat. Lu said to Rip, "Next time, the dog stays with you."

Marge asked, "Me?"

"No. Him."

Marge guessed, "The dog slept sideways in the middle of the bed."

"Yep."

"I should've known! A sly, clever dog, that way, slides past everything and does as he durned well wants. Just exactly like some men do."

So Lu nodded her head in an exaggerated up and down, once, in agreement.

Rip said to the dog, "You've blown it all for us

both. They know about you and they'll start wondering about me. It's all your fault.''

The dog laughed.

Marge and Lu asked in unison, "What about you?"

Without the blink of an eye and with earnest communication, Rip had the gall to look innocently at Lu and say, "I'm pure."

Both women went into uncontrolled laughter. That only made Marge surer that the two were sleeping together—without the dog.

The dog licked his paw and tidied his mostly black and some white fur coat. He knew they admired him.

Rip was patient with the female laughter. He told Lu firmly, "I left you here, alone, to sleep. That ought to show how careful I've been of you. I could have taken you out to my place."

Well, then, Lu sassed, "You said we'd barely get out there and have to turn back to get here in time for the afternoon visiting."

He tilted back his head to look at her and he commented, "So you remember that."

"I really thought I'd sleep on the back seat—out and back—and at least rest. Instead, the dog slept in the middle of my bed."

Marge and Hank said in unison, "Our bed." And Marge added, "You're just visiting."

Staunchly, with her nose up, Lu informed them, "While I was in the bed, it was mine."

Hank looked at Marge and said, "Oh-oh, she's one of them kind."

Marge straightened, "She's Rip's problem."

Rip sighed elaborately. "A man never has an out. Come on, woman, we'll try something else."

But she asked cautiously, "What?"

"Comb your hair and we'll go to the hospital so's you can rattle your brother and bring him out of his cozy little—"

She straightened at what might be criticism of her brother to say, "He knew Buddy."

Seeing her snap out of the doldrums to defend her brother, Rip tilted his head a little and just about almost smiled. He commented, "All people know any dog that seems friendly."

In a rush, unbottled words came from Lu. She said, "Nurses are strident. They speak loudly."

Rip nodded seriously, "I've noticed that. I think they have to be sure the patient can hear."

Lu went on, "They jerk draw-curtains and flip up blinds."

He agreed. "They have a lot to do."

"It's rude."

Rip said kindly, "In the daytime, people ought not to sleep. Then they aren't wakeful at night." It was obvious to him that she was not familiar with hospitals.

She looked aside thoughtfully, then she said, "Yes." She understood what he was saying.

Rip mentioned, "You've been asleep for almost two hours. Did it help? Other than the dog crowding you, did you sleep at all?"

"The whole, entire time." Lu just naturally said all that. TEXANS tend to elaborate. It's probably because they're the biggest state, other than Alaska, which TEXANS vow is mostly ice. So with the coming change of the global warming, Alaska will melt. Then TEXAS will be the biggest state again.

However, if it gets hot enough for *Alaska* to melt, TEXAS will be seared and probably vacant. No one'll give a hoot in hell which is bigger. The only TEXANS left to see it will be fried.

Saying goodbye to Marge and Hank was like saying goodbye to kin. They'd see them again. Marge said, "Come tomorrow and sleep. Don't bring the damned dog."

Buddy laughed. He actually did. That's why God saw to it that dogs, although they do try, don't actually talk in words to humans. Not understanding what dogs say, one can live with their comments.

The only thing that saves people from dogs taking over is the opposable thumb. If dogs had thumbs, they'd be in control. People would have to learn the dogs' language and tolerate their control.

Imagine a man sitting out and howling to the moon. Well, actually, some do, even now.

And men think women are strange.

Actually, to men, it's women who are strange. Women baffle men.

Rip looked over at Lu. She was magic. He wanted her. She made his body hurt and his eyes squinch. She wasn't ready.

She needed more time. Why did women need time? Why couldn't they be open enough to just say, "Okay"? Why did they need preliminaries first? Why did they have to make a man sweat it?

After they were comfortable and relaxed together, he'd ask her.

Maybe.

If she was like other women, she'd want to know how many other women he'd had and where were they now? It took experience for a man to know how to handle a woman. He wondered how "experienced" a man had to be before he didn't blunder and ruin everything.

Living wasn't easy.

Women were another problem entirely.

Driving to the hospital, Rip glanced at her body in the soft material. It took a while for him to actually see that she wore clothing, and it took a little longer to realize her clothing was uniquely subtle and probably very expensive.

He gradually understood that he couldn't afford her. She was beyond his touch. Her family was wealthy.

But being the man he was, Rip altered his thinking. Maybe she got her clothes at house sales or auctions. Maybe she just had good taste and knew what looked like magic on her. The gently colored, soft material was beautiful on her body. No, it was her body that was beautiful. It would be so under gunnysacks.

He squeezed his eyes as the want concentrated in his body, and he was silent.

With the change in hospital rules, Buddy got to go inside again. Everybody smiled at the dog.

The visitors went up the stairs to the third floor because elevators weren't something the dog had experienced. They didn't want to rattle him.

Andrew slept.

That bothered his sister. Lu asked the nurse, "Is he coming along all right?"

"Yes."

"He's sleeping."

"He opened his eyes in the night. He—maybe—watched the news on CNN. Don't worry about him."

But Buddy went over to the bed and put his paws up on the side as he said, "Wuff" quietly.

Again Andrew's hand came around and over to the back of the dog's head. There, Andrew's fingers moved on the dog's head. Then his hand went back to lie on the bed.

The dog then looked at Lu as if to say, *"See? He's not out of it."*

So Lu settled down and began to talk to her brother. It is said that a sleeping person will eventually respond if someone talks to him. So Lu told Andrew what all was happening. Who Rip was. How Rip had found him. And that Andrew was all right. The hospital was taking good care of him. And there was the straw by his cheek and he was to drink five swallows.

He must have heard. Standing next to Lu, Rip watched as Andrew turned his head, opened his mouth and took the straw into his mouth as his sister counted to five. But Andrew sucked five more sips from the straw.

How like Andrew. A courteously stubborn man who didn't automatically follow directions. He was self-directed. He'd be a nuisance to anyone who tried to guide him, at all.

The room phone flashed.

Since she was holding Andrew's hand, Lu indicated Rip should answer the phone.

He picked it up and said, "Andrew Parsons's room."

A female voice asked, "Who's this?" When Rip told the woman his name, she said, "I'm so glad to hear your voice. This is Andrew's mother. You're the one who found him. Thank you."

But Rip denied that, "It was the dog. It was Buddy. I just got him where he wanted to go, back across the plain. Why was Andrew there?"

"Heaven only knows. He's very like his father and a complete puzzle. To be the mother of such a strange person is rather boggling."

Rip laughed softly in his throat with such humor.

Mrs. Parsons inquired, "Is there anything Andrew needs? Is he awake?"

"Let me see if I can wake him."

"Oh, no—"

But being the kind of man he was, Rip told Mrs. Parsons, "It's daytime, and he ought to sleep at night. The nurse thinks he watches the midnight news."

"How typical. Put the phone by his ear, and I'll tell him so."

So Lu watched as Rip put the phone by Andrew's ear with the phone's mouthpiece available for a reply.

They both could hear Mrs. Parsons's voice and they saw Andrew's smile. But his eyes stayed closed and he didn't vocally respond.

Rip took the phone and said, "Here's your daughter." And he gave the phone to her.

"Mamma..." And she listened. She smiled. She

chuckled. She said, "I love you, too." Then she gave Rip the phone to put back.

Rip asked Lu, "Are your parents okay?"

"They think they'll be able to come out in a week or so. Even though Daddy gets worked up over his ailments, he really doesn't like hospitals. His parents, my grandparents, were in a terrible car wreck. They lingered for some time. My daddy was a young man and he became very allergic to hospitals."

"They died?"

"Not for quite a while. The doctors and nurses were devastated. They wanted them alive. They felt defeated."

"Ah." Rip understood then the strange reaction of the parents and why they hadn't rushed out there to their child who had become a stupid, illogical man. Rip looked down at the sleeping Andrew on the bed, and Rip was determined to be around and initiate the man into logic and carefulness.

Without actually knowing what Rip was thinking, Lu thoughtfully mentioned, "He's a Rhodes Scholar."

By some chance, Rip knew what one was and how a man got such a learning. But this man, there on the bed, needed some basic rules for himself. He'd get it from another man whose teaching was flying—and survival.

Who should walk into that hospital room, just then, but Tom Keeper! The dog went to him and Tom leaned down to say, "Hello, boy. You better?"

And the dog said sounds as he looked into Tom's eyes.

Rip was silent. It is a strange happenstance when

a man feels in control of a situation and his boss walks into the room.

Tom had come into the room as if he owned it. He smiled at Lu and said, "Hello, I'm Tom Keeper. I was here earlier."

Lu smiled. "I remember."

Then Tom saw Rip and exclaimed with a big smile, "Well, hello, Rip. Glad to see you. Everything okay?"

Rip just nodded.

Tom added, "Thank you for being such a help to the Parsons family." Then he told Lu, "You probably already know that it was Rip who took Buddy up in his plane to search for and find your brother. They did it just right."

Lu said, "You're the one who knew Buddy was looking for help."

Tom said seriously, "I have no idea why I turned the way I did. But the horse was curious and watching out beyond. I looked out over the land in such a way that I saw that little black dot. It was a miracle that I saw him at all. I had a fresh horse and I could have just...left. I'm not sure how the dog would have found anyone else. He was at the end of his rope. It was Rip who solved everything."

Rip said, "I just obeyed orders."

Tom laughed. "Orders? When have you ever had to have orders? You're always a way ahead of the rest of us and know exactly what to do. You can fly that plane in anything the weather tries us on. You're a miracle."

Tom was so earnest that Rip was very touched. And for Tom to have said all that in front of Lu! But then from the bed, the cracked voice said, "Amen," in agreement.

Andrew didn't even open his eyes, but he'd heard. The dog was still stretched up with his paws on the bed, and Andrew's hand was on the side of the dog's head. But his hand was lax and the man's breathing was sleep breathing. Had he actually said the word?

They'd all heard it.

Rip considered them all and then he said with a slight grin, "I think I ought to have a ribbon...or maybe a medal?"

Tom loved it.

Quite solemnly, Lu said, "Yes."

From the bed came the same word from Andrew. He, too, said, "Yes."

That made Lu's eyes fill. She smiled and looked at Rip. His regard was gently on her. He'd been knighted by her already. Her gratitude was obvious. To have her want a medal for him showed how she loved her family.

Tom suggested, "When Andrew's better, we'll have a big barbecue and invite the whole area."

From the bed, Andrew said, "Yes."

Tom laughed and went to the bedside. "Get well, Andrew. We need you there for everybody to gawk at and whisper about. They'll all chide you and give you all kinds of advice on how to tackle this land— alone. That's what galls the hell out of them, you were alone."

The slow lips said, "Buddy."

Tom agreed, "He saved your neck."

After a while, the man managed, "Yeah."
The dog's throat replied to some extent.
The man said, "Hush."
And they all laughed.

Three

———

On the hospital bed with his leg stabilized, Andrew Parsons seemingly went back into deep sleep, and it didn't matter if those in the room talked or laughed or even if they told sly jokes. They wouldn't get him to again respond to anything.

Considering the patient, Rip mentioned in a rather irritated manner, "By now, he's too used to sleeping days and—mentally—roaming nights. He's off-kilter."

Tom Keeper added, "A lot of adults do that. It depends on their business. What's Andrew's?"

Lu replied, "He's a writer and explorer. He feels the necessity to explore everything and tell people what they already know. He is of another time."

Tom Keeper laughed, but it was gently. He told her, "We are all of varying times. It's interesting to see and listen to the others. Andrew is not at all strange. He's one of us.''

Lu was inclined to agree, ''He's always endured and tolerated.''

Rip squinted his eyes and turned his head as if listening. Then he asked, ''Doesn't that sound just like a younger sister who doesn't feel like she's getting her share of attention?''

Lu surprised him. She said, ''Yep.'' Then she explained, ''Since he's okay, he may well recover and get to keep his left leg and, that way, I can be more critical.''

Then she moved to look at her brother's face to see if he'd heard, but he was peaceful and quiet.

His attitude didn't give any real hint that Andrew was out of it. He was sly and curious so he could pretend to be in deep sleep and unaware but, actually, he could be listening avidly.

With her comment on Andrew's leg, Rip asked carefully, ''His...leg?''

She nodded and looked at Rip with a hostile/brave mix. She needlessly explained, ''The one that was under the horse.''

Of course, Rip had been there, first, and he'd seen how Andrew had been trapped with his left leg under the dead horse. She had not. She had learned of it from the crew who'd removed the dead horse and rescued her brother.

Tom Keeper shifted his feet and kept his eyes on them as he said, ''The doctors seem to think there's hope.'' Then he looked up at Lu and smiled as he told the two visitors, ''I'll be back. Take care of yourselves, and if I can be of any help, please call me.

Here's my card or just ask Rip. I'll be sure to let him know where I'll be.''

Tom left slowly and Lu followed him to the room's door.

Rip couldn't believe Tom would actually leave! Especially as Rip was plotting on how to get rid of Tom. Rip had watched as Lu had listened to Tom. He'd watched her smile at Tom. Tom was a man who could have any woman he wanted.

Did Tom want Lu? My God. Rip thought, what if Tom Keeper really wanted Lu Parsons?

Rip didn't actually know what to do then. There was no way he could compete with Tom Keeper over such a woman. Having seen Tom, Lu might not ever again really focus her attention on Rip.

However, Rip was responsible for the dog. He couldn't just walk on out, too. But he could come back when he wanted. He was in charge of Andrew's dog. A slow smile bloomed inside Rip. Yeah. He had the patient's dog! So he had the right to be there in the hospital.

And, besides the dog, Rip was assuming the responsibility of Lu. He frowned. What if he got in too deep with Lu, but she looked at Tom instead, what would Rip Morris do?

His skin shivered. Just think of that. He was so involved with thinking of that neophyte woman that his skin shivered at the idea of losing her to Tom Keeper! That was serious.

He hadn't even kissed her—yet—or held her close against him, feeling her female body against his own male one. He'd better be careful of this *want,* inside him. She could be frigid or mean-mouthed. Other than the fact that she looked perfect, he really didn't know anything about her, at all!

Without his permission, Rip looked over at the budding woman. God. She was wonderfully made. She was something to see. She probably was a stickler, and she could be a stingy, mean-mouthed sass.

She hadn't been so far. Well, she'd been typically sisterlike in trying to talk with her sleeping brother. That was predictable.

Rip sneaked another look at her. Damn. She really was magic. She was—ethereal. He could just sit and stare at her…in between times.

He groaned silently. How could a man—like him—compete with Tom Keeper?

For his own sake, Rip needed to seem okay. Level. Solid. He shouldn't indicate he was panicked by another man. He ought to do something casual as if he was in control. A man who appeared in control could generally take control.

What had he and Lu been talking about? Andrew, of course. Rip looked over at the low sling that stabilized and protected Andrew's leg. Rip hadn't known the therapists who came and worked on Andrew. It couldn't be any fun for any of them.

He started to say something to Lu about her brother, but then he remembered that the sly Andrew apparently could hear if he wanted to. And with his eyes closed, nobody knew whether Andrew was listening. They wouldn't have any idea, unless Andrew said something.

So Rip didn't go on in talking to Andrew's sister about the harmed leg or ask any questions. Instead,

Rip moved slowly and watched his feet as men do when they are thinking carefully.

Right then, a cheerful, slender, awesome-looking, redheaded nurse came into Andrew's room and grinned at the silent couple. She went to Andrew. Without tact at all, and in a normal voice, the nurse said, "It's time to wake up and enjoy the day. Wake up."

Andrew sighed.

The nurse was busy with a thermometer and pulling the sheets free. She was arranging Andrew as if he was a rigid, man-sized rag doll who was her responsibility. She was so darling to see that she had undoubtedly been assigned to the single man to stir his interest in being alive.

In changing his position, she'd gasp and work to arrange him, and she'd need the patient's help. A sly push to force the patient into helping her.

She shook her head at Rip who moved to help. She told the silent patient, "You weigh a ton. Move to your side. This side."

And very slowly, Andrew did turn!

Well, why wouldn't he? She was bent over, pulling on his shoulder and hip and by turning, he could peek down the neck of her white uniform! That was a stimulation for any single man.

Even Rip could see that. But for himself, he discreetly looked away—mostly in order to see if Lu was monitoring him.

She was. She looked patient. She went over to the bed and said, "Tell me how I can help."

But as the nurse adjusted Andrew's leg in the sling,

she grinned and said, "I'm supposed to be able to do this all by myself. They tell me that it builds muscle. I can then defend myself. The doctors told me I was allowed to do this for my own good." She tilted her head, licked her smile and looked at Lu with a precious expression.

She made Lu grin.

Nurses are taught all kinds of sly things to help lift the spirits of the patient families. The staff is so positive. The surprise is, they mean it! They are determined the patient will be all right, by George, and they'll fight the devil to the brink.

Then the nurse untied the covering on Andrew's shoulder and rubbed something soothing on the skin on the exposed part of his back. He said, "Ummmmm."

In surprise, the nurse asked, "That feels nice? Nobody ever did this for me!"

There was an amused chuff of air in Andrew's nose. The nurse grinned and winked at the invalid's sister. Then she went on talking about what all was on the news and who all was there in the room and what all he'd have for the next meal. She added, "Be careful of the salad."

That's all that redheaded nurse said. She didn't say why he should be careful of the salad. Now what human person is going to ignore that cautioning? They are going to *look* at the meal on the tray. They're going to be curious. They'll probably even taste a little of it. They'll know the hospital won't poison them. What could possibly be wrong with the salad?

It was, of course, another sly little nudge to make the patient curious...and eat.

Rip had decided that while the little redhead was something and would be around for a while so that he could get acquainted with her, he was actually more interested in Lu. He couldn't risk Lu getting peeved with him. So he gave her his attention.

Lu asked, "What is it about nurses that is so attractive?"

Rip bit into his lower lip in some obvious consideration. And having considered the woman before him quite seriously, he inquired of Lu, "What... nurses?"

With great tolerance, Lu explained kindly, "Like the one who was just in this room."

And damned if he didn't look around as if he'd not noticed the redhead leaving and was looking for someone other than the patient, Lu or himself. He looked puzzled as if he didn't quite understand. He inquired, "Hmmm?"

Lu could have swatted him. "She must have really knocked you off center." She said that in disgust.

"Who? Are you talking about the nurse who was just here?" He shook his head slowly. "Not that nurse? She was efficient and knew what she was doing."

"So you did notice that redhead."

"What redhead?"

"The nurse."

With such innocence but with concern in communication, Rip asked, "The one who was here to care for your brother? She had red hair?'' He was pleasantly curious.

"What were you looking at on her, if you couldn't see her red hair?"

And earnestly, Rip said, "I saw your brother turned and helped."

From the bed, her brother just about choked. He was turned on his side so he couldn't choke, therefore, Lu ignored him.

But Rip went around the bed with the dog, and they both looked at the face of Andrew Parsons. The dog stretched up with his forefeet on the bed, and Rip was bending over to see into the harmed man's face.

He was awake and his eyes were dancing with laughter.

Since Rip didn't think the accusations were humorous, he frowned at the patient and said, "He's probably stopped up and needs a cathartic."

The smile left Andrew's face and he looked appalled.

The dog talked to the man with odd noises deep in his throat. He was trying to communicate. That was a problem with Andrew. He didn't want his sister talking to him and worrying at him, so he whispered, "Hush," to the dog and to the stranger there by him.

The dog was obedient; the man understood. They were silent. Andrew closed his eyes and his face was still.

It was right then that Lu came around the bottom of the bed and looked at her brother. His eyes were closed and he was, indeed, still.

Lu asked the man and the dog, "Why did you two come around to this side of the bed?"

The dog was safe, he could look at the woman and reply honestly, but she wouldn't understand the dog's sounds. Rip was open-faced and serious. "I thought I heard him say something. That nurse was pretty rough. I just wanted to be sure he was okay."

Now what was Lu to reply to a recent stranger who spoke with such earnest kindness?

The dog's odd bark covered the strangled sound from her brother who was allegedly in a deep sleep and lying so still on the bed.

Watching him soberly, Lu said to Rip, "I beg your pardon."

Leading the sister to the door, Rip said, "You've had a tough time. You must be very tired. I hadn't realized that when you tried to sleep, the dog wouldn't stay on the floor for you. I've gotten used to sharing my bed with him. I wonder if your brother has let the dog sleep with him? The dog acts like it's his privilege."

That type of chatter is called changing the subject.

Lu was open about it. She said, "Andrew isn't very adult. It wouldn't surprise me, at all, if he sleeps on the floor and just gives the dog the bed. Maybe Buddy thinks that, with you, he's the guest and you're sharing his bed!"

Seeming to look down at Lu, Rip's eyes turned back under his lashes and he saw Andrew slide a quick hand over his mouth. It was well done.

The three visitors left Andrew's room and went down the hall to let the dog visit with the hospitalized boy. Chuck was exuberant just that the dog came into the room. Chuck didn't even see the adults who didn't count. And of course, Buddy had already understood he was the prime visitor there, too.

As he'd done before, the dog put his front feet up on the boy's bed and visited with throat sounds that humans have never really understood. A whole lot of people have never realized the fact that dogs have a perfectly good language for a higher echelon of beings. Humans will eventually get to that stage…dogs hope.

Besides being a loner by his strange upbringing, Rip's job of flying was mostly solitary. He observed and reported by a page of observations or, on occasion, there were pages of a report on the same subject, depending on what was happening that he could assimilate from the air.

Confronted by communication with actual people was a slow and sorted-out awkward guess for Rip. Being a loner had never bothered him before then. To fly was a miracle and worth the isolation.

But now, there was Lu. He felt privileged just to occasionally glance at her. To see her. To look at her mouth. At her body…but not too often or he'd go on overload. He was zonked.

He breathed slowly and deeply for control. That was better than panting.

The dog Buddy panted. He was laughing at Rip. He knew Rip's problem.

Rip understood the dog was aware of his need for Lu. The dog wasn't even subtle in his humor.

Well, it did amuse Buddy that the man took such caution and delayed for no real reason. It was obvious the woman wanted Rip. What was the problem? Humans are very strange.

There was no one around Rip who could find out if Lu was interested in another man, or committed to somebody else. There was no one to ask except the sly fox who was her brother, over there, on the bed, pretending to be out of it.

Even Rip thought people were a little off-kilter. He understood Buddy's hilarity. Obviously, knowing all that, Buddy was tolerant of Andrew because the dog could understand humans were...odd.

In the silent room, Rip wondered if he went into a coma would Lu sit by him and worry about him? Naw. For him, a coma would be a waste of time. He didn't want to lie helpless in a bed with his eyes closed. He wanted to watch her.

Lu was magic. And that's as far as his thinking got that was printable. After that, Rip just looked at Lu and his thoughts were triple X-rated. Maybe five *X*'s. His eyes were hooded by his lashes and he breathed very carefully so's not to alert her to his lust.

She was alerted. She was controlling her own reaction to Rip. She was exceptionally casual. That should have been a clue for him, right there. She didn't seem to even look at Rip, but she looked.

His hands were in his pant pockets.

She said, "I brought some playing cards, but I don't really care about playing solitaire. Would you like to play gin or bridge or—"

"Poker. My deal."

She thoughtfully slid out a stubborn or maybe an eye-catching lower lip. "We'll draw for dealer."

He won.

* * *

She should have noted how he handled the cards. He was not a novice. He was slick. He dealt five cards each. He picked his up and spread them tightly, holding them in his big hands. They bet up to ten matches.

She had no chance, at all, of seeing his cards. But then she was no slouch at poker. At least she considered that she and Rip were close to equal in poker. She underestimated him.

They ignored the patient, they didn't whisper. They played a battle game that was riveting. They argued and gasped and laughed. People stopped off and peeked in the doorway to see what all was happening with male and female voices laughing thataway.

And her brother was irritated because he was using the coma shield to keep everyone else at bay. He was competitive, and the innocent game was stirring his interest and making him restless to be involved. People are really nasty, interfering in a man's life.

Andrew could understand that nurses and sisters are really an irritation to male patients. Sisters talk and nurses don't get into bed, alongside a needy patient.

Mothers are preferable because they're generally concerned. His daddy had taken his mother's attention from Andrew by being his usual panicked self. His father was a ham, and his mother was a pushover for his dad.

What was his sister doing hanging around? If she wasn't there, Andrew could be playing poker with the pilot—whatever his name was. Andrew never much paid any attention to other people's names.

Andrew was somewhat self-centered. He was... considerably self-centered. Actually, he thought he was the only reason the world was as it was, and it was for him. He was the center of the universe.

A good many people feel that way about their position in time. Andrew wasn't at all unusual.

But neither of the poker players even noticed that Andrew was restless and irritated. They did not hear his sighs. They were not caught by the subtle sounds of his movements.

They were concentrated on their own game, their competition, their snide minds working ahead. Across the small table, they smiled at each other as if each was topping the other.

The game between the two was cutthroat poker with matches as loot.

The nurse came in and looked at their small table. She was appalled! She asked softly but with her chin out and her eyes bugged out, "What are you two doing playing with—*matches!*"

She was like a mother hen, for Pete's sake. Rip replied logically, "We're playing poker. I knew you all would object to us playing with real money."

"Matches!" She repeated indignantly.

"Yeah." His reply was hesitant as he tried to figure her out.

"In a *hospital!* Do you know the conflagration such a stupid thing might do in this place?"

Rip looked around. "It's fireproof."

"Not the mattresses! Not the linens! Not the screenings of cloth or clothing! Do you realize what horror you could start with—matches?"

They gave up on matches. They used real money. The game was more intense. They'd both put in five dollars. Rip had it changed into pennies, nickles and dimes at the cafeteria down in the basement. It wasn't as much fun to play with real money...for her.

She won.

Rip congratulated her and took some of Andrew's flowers to make her a halo of flowers. It was hilarious. They snickered and gasped in hushing each other's laughter and indicating they should be quiet for the patient's sake.

Unfortunately, since he was pretending sleep, Andrew couldn't protest at all, but he ground his teeth.

It's really irritating when other people are in a man's hospital room, and pay no attention to him, at all, but just enjoy themselves.

Rip and Lu went out again for dinner at Marge and Hank's place. The two ate in the cafeteria on the first floor, and they never mentioned Lu was in any need of rest. However, the two talked to each other across the table the whole, entire time. They gestured and laughed and leaned toward each other. And they managed to lick their platters clean! With all that talk, they could eat...too! Amazing.

Marge told Hank, "Just look at them talking. What do you suppose they do the rest of the time?"

Hank replied, "I don' know."

And Marge's eyes squinted with knowledge. "They sure don't talk away from here. Just look at them—catching up—in talk!"

Hank laughed.

Marge nodded in agreement with herself and her eyes stayed squinted. She said, "They're getting acquainted. It's a little late, but at least they do have something to say to each other. It isn't all just sex.''

In blank-faced astonishment, Hank put in, ''What's wrong with sex?''

Marge just snipped, ''You animal.'' But she swished her hips as she walked away—and Hank watched after her. She knew he did so because she looked back. Women tend to do things like that.

Four

Of course, Marge did wonder if Rip and Lu would want to leave the downstairs dining rooms and go up to the guest room and…be…together. Marge sighed with some nostalgia of memories. She remembered how it'd been for her and Hank. She understood the two apparently couldn't get enough of each other. At least, at the table, they were talking and not just panting at each other, like dogs in heat.

That Rip really must be something if the girl had been so exhausted. Marge smiled and barely shook her head. She looked over at Hank and whispered, "We can't let 'em go on upstairs together to the room?" That's a TEXAS positive-negative questioning sentence which can be confusing to the listener.

Hank lifted inquiring eyebrows and asked, "How come we can't? We're not charging 'em anything for the room and what they do—behind a closed door—is their own business."

Marge smiled. She giggled. She licked her lips and shook her head. "To just allow them to close the door of the room, thataway, would be outrageous?" She was asking her husband to give an opinion.

Hank just laughed in his throat the old way that shivered Marge's surprised insides. She whispered, "Then you tell *him*. I just can't say anything like that to her and still pretend that I don't know what all they've been doing...and what all they'll do up there."

Hank's eyes danced with amusement. "Okay."

So Marge could be shocked and gasp, "You didn't even *think* about it, you just said 'okay' like you intended doing it thataway all along!"

And Hank said, "Yep."

He did.

Marge tilted back her head and asked, "You've been thinking about them needing a place alone?"

With his eyes on her, like old times, Hank asked softly, "Remember how we were that winter?"

But the winter memory, most assuredly, wasn't chilling because Marge just melted. "Yeah."

Hank hadn't seen her that vulnerable since before they were married. Hank sighed inside his body so's Marge didn't know how easy he was. But he smiled at her.

And she knew anyway.

As Rip paid their lunch bill, it was Hank who said to him, "Her room's ready. I'll put the dog on the back porch. You all can sleep without the dog in your bed, too.'' While Hank raised his eyebrows, he nodded a couple of times.

Hank had really startled Rip who didn't reply. He looked off to the side and then at his feet. He nodded again very soberly.

Rip wondered: Would she? Naw. She was of another echelon altogether. Being a pilot, he knew the word echelon. But he didn't know about a woman with her background. He and she didn't match.

Well, she was female and he was male, and they could match real well…if she was willing. This was just a little sudden for her. But who could tell if she might not be interested?

He'd find out. He almost smiled at Hank. Rip was too mature to giggle or huff. But he did just barely smile. That showed he wasn't a country boy, he had his city shine. He could handle just about anything.

He'd see if he could handle Lu.

Rip mentioned to Hank, "I'll tell her after we're upstairs. Thank you. I owe you a favor." That was the mature Rip. The room was without cost. Rip would return the favor in another way.

So he went to Lu who was talking to Marge who, in turn, watched her guest avidly and was stimulated by Rip's easy approach. His approach flustered Marge who *knew* what was coming along with the couple being in bed together, for an afternoon…nap! Yeah. Sure.

So Marge was a little joggled and her eyes danced and she looked beyond the couple to exchange a knowledgeable glance with her husband. Hank grinned.

Rip took Lu's elbow into one big hand and smiled

in a rather aloof manner at Marge. He said, "Thank you."

Marge blushed scarlet but she wiggled and became rather animated.

Lu added her thank-you. She said, "This is one of the best eating places I've ever been. And thank you for the nap yesterday. You saved my life. I hadn't known how exhausted I was, or how close I was to a collapse."

And Marge found herself replying, "Another nap will help you. I know Rip—"

But Lu laughed. "I slept like a log last night. I think it was because I was alone and without that dog taking up the whole bottom half of the bed! I'll sleep tonight, too. My brother is responding quite well, and I'm not as worried as I was. Did Rip tell you we played poker—"

And Marge's eyes widened as she saw them playing strip poker all—

"—today in Andrew's hospital room? I won! I really need to pay the lunch bill. I must have most of Rip's money!" She laughed.

Marge was sober-faced. Maybe shocked. "You're not going to take your nap…here?"

Lu replied, "I was so grateful yesterday to have that time to sleep here. I didn't even notice the dog had the whole, entire bottom of the bed—"

Marge urged, "The dog's outside on the porch. You can have the bed—"

"Why, thank you." But then Lu just went on, "I don't need a nap. I really slept, here, yesterday afternoon and then last night at the hospice. I've caught up."

In shock, Marge looked at Rip for some rebuttal, but he was sober-faced and his eyes were on Lu.

Marge wasn't at all sure how to help Rip. But Lu was saying, "You all have one of the best restaurants I've ever known. Thank you. And thank you for that respite yesterday. I was exhausted." Lu gently reached out and hugged the just about comatose Marge. Then Lu said, "I'll see you tomorrow."

And the two guests—left. They just walked on out of the house, retrieved the dog and went to Rip's pickup. Rip never said one word.

But then, neither did Marge or Hank comment to each other. They just watched the three get into the pickup and then drive carefully around to the street, and go on off down the way and out of sight.

Then Marge and Hank looked at each other in that same surprised shock.

Finally Hank soothed, "Next time."

Marge exclaimed, "She must be nuts!"

That made Hank laugh.

The three drove away. Rip, Lu and the dog. Rip mentioned, "We've got the time to drive out to the place, so's you can see it. Want to?"

"How do you have all this time?"

In the middle of perfect weather, Rip didn't mention the Keepers had released him to help the injured man. He just replied, "With this fog, we can't see anything, up that high, to fly."

"Fog?" She looked out the pickup's window at another clear day with sunshine.

He suggested, "Breathe on the window."

She leaned over and blew on the car window. There

isn't all that much moisture in the air clear out there in West TEXAS, all the time, so her breath didn't change anything, at all.

But Rip said, "See? It's all fogged up."

Her being from a rather odd family, anyway, it was no surprise to Rip when she said, "Oh," just like she accepted that it was foggy outside.

Rip mentioned with some regret, "Since you're not in bed, we have the time. We can go right on out to the Place, you can see where Buddy sleeps and you can see how the place works."

"That sounds exciting."

Rip slid a look over at her. The very idea of sleeping with her had triggered him quite seriously. She owed him a little time, being with him, even if it was just sitting on that side of the pickup's seat and looking around at the territory.

If she stayed around him, she'd get to be more comfortable with him and—who knows what all might still happen? Her brother was going to be a while in the local hospital. And since her brother was no longer critical, she had to visit him on schedule now, just like everybody else.

Right then, she was with him...with Rip Morris. She didn't have a whole lot of control. He was driving. He could convince her to go along and see the countryside. He did that.

She finally said, "Okay. This had better be interesting."

"You'll take to it." He said that with a smug TEXAS confidence.

She inquired, "Do all you West TEXANS around these here parts, think this place is heaven?" She gestured to take in the whole high, flat, fragile area with short mesquite trees, here and there, that had been windblown and gnarled. The trees were mostly left in draws to stop a surprise rush of the waters when wet weather takes away the precious soil.

Complacently TEXAN, Rip replied, "You'll understand the West TEXAS feeling in good time."

"What...good times do you have?"

"I meant that you'll eventually come to appreciate this land...and me." He took his eyes off the straight road and looked over at her in a way that scared her stomach. Well, it wasn't exactly scared, but it was a very odd feeling that she'd never before experienced. She wasn't sure if it was a good or a bad scared.

Whichever way it was, for her, Rip was casual and relaxed. She wondered how a man could be casual and relaxed having said something so alluring? What did he mean by her being appreciative of...him? That he could drive? That he could play poker? Or that he could play...with...her?

Just the idea of his playing with her gave her body a very intense, odd thrill. Her skin was alive and her nipples were puffed. She blushed.

She sat still and was careful. To help herself breathe, she took a big, deep breath and only then realized she had not exhaled first.

Inflated thataway, it was just a wonder that she didn't float off the pickup's seat and bang against the cab roof. She discreetly exhaled enough. Soon she felt she was sitting more solidly on the cab seat.

Being female, with a dangerous male, was very similar to being trapped. She was in his pickup truck, they were going out somewhere in the great beyond, and she had no control, at all, over him or over anything else.

Well, Marge and Hank knew she'd be with Rip.

She asked, "Where are we going?"

"Out to the Keeper place so's you can see where I live and where I'm keeping your brother's dog."

She was a little disappointed that he wasn't carrying her away to his lair. That sort of thought came from being kin to her father and brother who were just a little strange.

Could she have been flawed by several rampant genes from her dramatic father?

Surely not. She was her mother's child. She'd never had any of the yearnings to wonder and observe that plagued her daddy and brother. She had never needed to go see or listen to or know of strange peoples and their baffling thoughts of times and of other peoples.

She had never even once dreamed any of those yearnings to wonder and observe might crop up in…her. How astonishing. So here she was in the cab of Rip's pickup— He was named…Rip? Now, that was just plain weird. Who would name a child, Rip, for crying out loud! Why…Rip?

Well, she supposed it was better for a male to cope with such a name than for a female to be so branded. Just think what a man named—Rip—would do about naming children of his own! How sobering to think of that.

So she discarded him.

She would endure the day and not get involved with him ever again.

* * *

The Keeper ranch was about like anything else. If a person has seen the films about ranches, there is a great scale of where and how such people live. The Keeper place was moderate. It was old and cared for.

There were different types of trees and there were cherished pecan trees, but around the place the trees were mostly oaks. Some were quite tall and shaded most of the two-story houses. They spread out over the single-story houses.

How interesting that the trees' presence gave the observer knowledge. Riding along the area, a visitor wouldn't have seen such trees before they had arrived there at the Keepers' place. The oaks were a surprise. They had obviously been brought there and planted some long time ago. They had had long, careful care.

She said simply, "The oaks."

Rip looked at the precious trees. Then he explained, "They've been here for a couple of hundred years. When the Keepers bought this land from the Indians who lived here, they brought the oaks and planted them. The planted oaks didn't all live, but they just planted more. Those still here will last a couple of hundred more years.

"As you can see, the Keepers have planted other oaks along the way. That's security for the trees. It makes it easier for the Keepers to be sure to have enough of them. There are groves that were planted and fenced to protect them from the cattle until the trees are big enough to endure the herds."

"How—farsighted of them."

Honestly, Rip told her, "The Keepers are good people. Tom is especially nice. Even though he must have been ticked that Andrew was so stupid in traveling alone, he'd been courteous.

"Going out alone is a no-no up here." Rip explained. He was serious and open. There was no reason to smooth or soothe her. He went on, "It's probably a no-no everywhere now. Anybody who goes out on his own is being stupid."

She lifted her eyebrows. "Driving a truck or a car alone?"

He readily agreed, "Especially in this area. It depends on how traveled the roads are. These roads around here are pretty empty, two laned...or just tracks. If you were driving your car and it stopped and you had no water, it could be very serious, very soon."

She just said the words, "Cellular phones."

Rip nodded. "They're vital."

On the Keeper Compound, the pickup truck rolled to a stop by one particular house in the rather scattered bunch. The house was not large, but it had three oaks around it. The house was newly painted and neatly white. It was a one-story cottage with a porch and a porch swing. There were two rocking chairs on the porch.

She asked, knowing, "Whose house is this? It's certainly well kept."

"It's one of the Keeper's houses for the crew. This is my house. Because I fly a plane and have a different sleeping schedule, I got the house to myself. If you'll notice, this is one of the smaller places."

"It's charming." And she smiled at the house.

Rip had thought she'd keep her eyes on the Keepers' big, old, two-story house that sprawled out over the land. She hadn't even mentioned it. They would go there for supper that night, and Rip would see how she responded to the difference in the houses.

He would see if she accepted the automatic invitation to stay there or if she stayed with him. It would be a test. Which would she do? And if she stayed with him... Would she want a room to herself? She might.

If she stayed at his place and wanted a separate room, he could handle that. He could handle it if she wanted to stay at the big house. He would just see what she chose. Yeah. And his body groaned.

His home was no modern condo. Its one floor contained a living room, dining room, kitchen, two bedrooms and a complete bathroom. With anything that far out from repair, there was a neat, emergency outhouse in the backyard surrounded by lacy mesquites.

Because of the sometime cyclones, there was a basement with two entrances. One entrance was from the house with stairs down to it, and the other exit was out of the side of the house's basement with doors that opened upward on those stairs.

Taking note of the basement door, she inquired, "Cyclones?"

And he grinned. "So you're an actual TEXAN?"

"How'd you guess that?"

His face was so vulnerable. "You said 'cyclone' when the Yankees have changed the word to 'tornadoes.'"

She said, "Yankees are pushy."

And he exclaimed in shock, "I've noticed that very thing!"

He made her laugh.

It was interesting to him that she looked around with interest, but she was in no hurry to go to the big house. She went outside and looked at the emergency yard pump. But then she went into the kitchen and turned on the faucet. It also worked. So she just lifted her eyebrows at Rip for an explanation.

He gave that easily. "The yard pump is like the other cyclone cellar stair, or the outhouse. We're just cautious."

Now it was very interesting to hear a man—who was new in that old, old place—speak of the place as if he was a part of it all. The Keepers must be unusual.

That was the first time Lu felt any curiosity about the Keepers. She'd already met Tom at the hospital and spoken with him easily enough. Now she noted the basic caution and planning his ancestors had figured out.

This was especially so since her own family was rather inept. They had never looked ahead nor planned for care, even of themselves. Her brother Andrew was a good example. Of course, he had taken the dog along on his trek, and he had had food and water. Not enough water, of course, out on that tableland, but he had had a canteen.

She asked Rip, "What do you take along in your plane for survival?"

He did blink. He was still looking at the house. He was trying to find a way to mention his painting it. And she wanted to know about plane...survival?

He replied, "We have water in a survival kit, radio, covering and a rifle and handgun. There are some odd creatures around here."

"Creatures? The deer and the antelope?"

"Snakes." He turned out a hand to include the area. "The real kind and then there's the human kind."

"Ahhh."

"One of our pilots was shot down by some clown. We've never found out who. If it hadn't been for the signal contact, we might have lost him."

She just watched Rip soberly.

"There's all kinds of jealousy," Rip explained. "We're very fortunate, here, and we all work together. We are very like the ancient castles with high walls. Our walls are our eyes. Our rifles. Our radio links. We seldom have any problem at all. But we are careful. We are so alert that we can mostly stop anything invasive before it really starts. That's one reason there are planes here."

She frowned. "How terrible to have to be that careful."

"Cheating has been going on through all the times of man. One way or another. It's still here. Are you infiltrating to get our loot? Our cattle?"

She gave him a patient, exasperated look but she said, "You caught me in time."

"I'll make you...see the light."

She watched him, wondering what he'd almost said...first.

It was interesting that only then did the dog go outside. He went through a topside, swinging door that was just his size. He moved quickly so the swinging door didn't swat his backside.

Lu went over to the window and watched as the dog, Buddy, stood at the top of the porch steps and looked out, on beyond. He lifted his nose and sniffed what the breeze carried.

As Lu watched the dog, she realized Rip was close behind her. She immediately understood he was on overdrive and his breathing was being carefully controlled.

She moved aside and casually looked at the furniture. She found he was moving to block her. How clever men are. She looked at him point-blank and saw they were only about a yard apart. She asked, "Do you have a garden? Vegetables?"

He considered her soberly, then he smiled just a little but his eyes danced. He replied, "Glad you asked. Come look."

The dirt was fragile, but the Keepers were really keepers of the land. They used all the vegetable leftovers and animal deposits and put it back into the soil. The gardens were rich. The growth was satisfactory.

Rip mentioned that they seldom watered. That was interesting. So they grew vegetables which didn't need help. The chance rains were enough. With the mesquites controlled, there was ground water enough for the other trees.

So Lu had seen the house and garden. She looked beyond and saw the endless solid land. One could hardly ask to go out to see that land. It was out there before her and changeless. She did look. A person alone there, would feel isolated.

With curiosity, she asked Rip, "When you fly, what do you see?"

And he shifted his feet carefully so that he could consider her question. She was already feeling—isolated? Alone? He was with her. He was right there, near to her.

His careful reply was, "We look for specific things. We don't look at the panorama so much as we look for thieves or for cattle rustlers...in big vans along the roads. Once a van was covered with mesquite branches. Had to be city fellas, doing that, we couldn't believe anybody would be that dumb."

"It was that obvious?"

"Yeah."

"What do you do when you just see an actual van parked along the way?"

He explained, "We call in and the state police go by and ask if they need help."

"That could be chancy for the cops."

Rip shook his head. "They know what they're doing—and we're flying overhead at the same time. With the flatland there's stable landing room close by, and we can follow them if they only move a ways."

Lu nodded. "I'd think that would be discouragement enough."

"It is...mostly. Some yahoo always tries something. The thing we hate the most is their cutting the fences. That irritates us so much that we get a little cranky."

She smiled at his word choice but she agreed, "I can understand that."

"I landed once and was mending a fence enough that the cattle couldn't get through there before a crew came along to fix it, and a cop's car stopped. He thought he'd caught me. That I had been cutting the fence lines and was pretending to be putting them back together.

"I had a hell of a time convincing him, because there wasn't anybody on the home line. So he just watched me put it all together, which I was doing *anyway,* and he took my flying license to check it out. I was irritated as all bloody hell."

Lu watched Rip. She said softly, "You must have had him scared spitless."

Rip admitted, "He was jerky, but he was earnest. I think the earnestness and commitment he showed was what made me tolerate him."

"I'm glad you did."

He mentioned earnestly, "Cops scare the s-s-s-spit out of me."

So she asked, "What all have you done?"

"Nothing!" He shook his head. "Not lately. There was a time when I'd thumbed my nose at them, but that was back before I realized how rough their lives are and how asinine budding males can be."

"You're adult."

He grinned at her. "Finally."

That was probably when she began to love him. She smiled back at him and she laughed softly in her throat in a way that lifted the hair on his scalp and shivered him intimately. She was a treasure.

Was he ready for a woman who would be a treasure? How could he know she could even *look* at him? Could she? Could she touch him? Could she lie against him and allow him to touch her? Could she love him?

Just asking such questions was an indication of how far gone he was already. That was scary.

He asked her with a clear face, "Are you gonna make me a molasses pecan pie? Every female guest has to do that. It's the rule.'' He nodded with his words.

She inquired, ''Do you have the recipe?''

''Uh-oh. You don't know how to make such a pie? That's—serious.'' He was naked-eyed and solemn.

She laughed.

And he watched her laugh. She shivered his vitals and filled his chest. How could that be…so, in such a short time? He was that susceptible? Surely not. But he looked at her seriously and was mesmerized.

She saw the dog off to one side and asked, ''How do you call him?''

''We whistle. Can you whistle thataway without needing to use your fingers?''

She lifted her nose, took a deep breath and gave a whistle which could be heard at—maybe—thirty feet.

He sighed with great tolerance, then he told her, ''Hold your fragile ears, I'll call the dog.'' Then he asked, ''Why do you want him?''

She gestured with her hand. ''Well, he's all by himself, out there, and I thought he might be lonesome. I was going to let him know we are outside.''

''Honey, he already knows that, and he doesn't care. If you need him for some reason or the other, that's a whole different angle from just calling him to see if he'll come where you are. You gotta have a reason or he won't come the next time you whistle for him.''

She looked off at the dog who was busy and curious and looking around. He did not need to be called to them at all. They didn't need him for anything and he was looking around for his own reasons. Rip was right. They ought not call the dog just to make him come to them. She understood.

But Rip then said, "If *you* need the dog for any reason, you call him. He'll protect you. If someone you don't like is near you, call the dog. He'll understand. He won't attack anyone unless he realizes it's needed."

Lu heard the words and listened carefully. "Is there a particular whistle to tell that information to the dog?"

"Just whistle and wave him to you. Or just yell at him, and he'll come. I found that out right away. Your brother trained him well. The only thing Andrew hadn't taught him was to go and get somebody to help them. Buddy did that on his own. It had never occurred to Andrew that he couldn't do everything his way and get by. Did you know the horse was shot?"

"Who—" She gasped and looked at Rip in shock.

"We don't know how or who. But the horse was shot. I didn't know until the others came back to our place. It could have been a stray bullet that just went wide. We are trying to find out who it was. None of our people was out on the plateau. We're trying to find out who might have been there. I saw nobody when I went with Buddy out to find Andrew. As you've probably heard, it had been over two days that Andrew had been trapped under that horse. We'll have a time backtracking that one. Finding out can well be never. But we're trying."

"I thought the horse fell."

"It did. Right after it was shot. A hell of a big bullet. We will be very curious what anyone with that sort of gun was doing out there on Keeper land."

"That's scary."

Rip asked, "Nobody told you?"

"No." She was wide-eyed. "They probably thought they'd wait until Andrew was cognizant."

"He is now."

She was indignant. "He's out cold. In shock or something."

Kindly, Rip told her, "He's a loner and hates casual conversation. It bores him."

"Now, how in the world do you know that?"

"I've seen him. The dog covers for Andrew's laughs."

She commanded, "Whistle for Buddy, I have to talk to him."

"How you gonna do that?"

"I'll think of something."

"It'd be best if you practice calling him yourself. Try it."

And she did, several times. The only reason the dog came to her is that he saw her trying to use her fingers in her mouth to make her whistle clearer.

Five

What Rip had said, about average and especially really smart dogs being aloof and craftily hard to control, was just about right. But then, dogs understand women probably better than men understand women. So when Buddy heard the thin little whistle that was almost beyond even a dog's hearing, he turned and looked at the woman to be sure it had been she who'd called him.

It was, indeed, she. So the dog watched awhile, and she did gesture for him as she gave that same nothing whistle. Buddy thought women were not only strange but pushovers and worth the time they took because they did tend to pet the dogs and give them morsels of odd food. Being indulged was one of the pluses in tolerating humans.

Humans were easy. A dog could pull just about any

trick on a human. When dogs panted, they were laughing.

There were men whose thinking was very similar to a dog's thinking when it came to a human female, but a man's thinking was for another reason.

Rip stood there with his thumbs in the outside corners of his pant pockets in the casual, tolerant manner of a man who is waiting for a woman to look at him and see him. He is always sure she will do that, and he is almost generally right.

Women are a trial to a man.

Worthwhile! Sure. Just about always. But it takes…so…much…*time!*

Buddy came up within talking range and hesitated to see if the woman was still serious or just being female.

She snapped her fingers and made a noise with her lips to get the dog's attention. It wasn't a whistle or a command, but just to get Buddy's attention.

Buddy was tolerant, but he just watched the female to see what she had in mind and if she was hiding a leash that would trap him into boredom.

Being idle, Rip picked up a knot of wood and examined it before he pitched it toward the nearest tree trunk to get it out of the way of the humongous weed mower.

Well, without even thinking, the dog fetched back the knot of wood! That was a surprise for both of the humans. They were delighted. The dog found he'd made a mistake, but he was so amused by the humans' exclamations that he went and got their thrown wooden knot any number of times.

Finally, Rip threw it far enough that the dog pretended he couldn't find it. He went through the grasses and appeared to try to earnestly look for it. But he went by the knot several times, knowing it was there, every time, and avoiding it.

So, since the dog had really searched, the humans looked in a farther area. The dog sat and panted. The humans allowed that because he'd been very diligent in searching, and they thought he was tired. He was laughing.

The humans could not find the knot of wood. They finally came back to the dog who had judiciously moved over several yards from the actual wooden knot and just lay panting. What a fake he was.

But the two humans bragged on him and petted his head. The man did it in a regular way and his voice didn't change, but the woman's voice and words were different. She just about cooed.

That made the dog's laughter a little worse. He had 'em.

But the urge to show off isn't entirely human. What did Buddy instinctively do to show off? He ran around a little, and then he did an impulsive, reckless back flip! And he instantly knew it had been a mistake. They'd urge for more. And of course, they did! They exclaimed and bragged on him, and he did it again!

People aren't the only ones who show off.

It was Rip who finally said, "Buddy's had enough exercise." The dog hadn't, actually, but Rip was bored just watching the dog garner all Lu's attention. Jealousy is odd.

So the dog sat down and was smart enough to pant

GET A FREE TEDDY BEAR...

You'll love this plush, cuddly Teddy Bear, an adorable accessory for your dressing table, bookcase or desk. Measuring 5 ½" tall, he's soft and brown and has a bright red ribbon around his neck – he's completely captivating! And he's yours *absolutely free*, when you accept this no-risk offer!

AND TWO FREE BOOKS!

Here's a chance to get **two free Silhouette Desire® novels** from the Silhouette Reader Service™ absolutely free!

There's no catch. You're under no obligation to buy anything. We charge nothing – ZERO – for your first shipment. And you don't have to make any minimum number of purchases – not even one!

Find out for yourself why thousands of readers enjoy receiving books by mail from the Silhouette Reader Service. They like the **convenience of home delivery**...they like getting the best new novels months before they're available in bookstores...and they love our **discount prices!**

Try us and see! Return this card promptly. We'll send your free books and a free Teddy Bear, under the terms explained on the back. We hope you'll want to remain with the reader service – but the choice is always yours!   (U-SIL-D- 04/98)   **225 SDL CF4R**

NAME		
ADDRESS		APT.
CITY	STATE	ZIP

Offer not valid to current Silhouette Desire® subscribers. All orders subject to approval.

NO OBLIGATION TO BUY!

as if he'd been overworked. That panting is one of a sly dog's tricks.

To catch Lu's attention to himself, Rip asked her, "Do you like seeing far? Or are you a ruined woman of the cities?"

So Lu looked out over that vast, empty, tilled and cared-for land. She tilted her head and told Rip, "It's the subtle colors that catch my eye. This would make a wonderful watercolor." And she moved a hand out to indicate the flat land on beyond.

To encourage her talking and to take her mind from the dog, Rip asked, "You a painter?"

"I am, but it is of the Fine Arts."

With such a reply, Rip thought something rather remotely akin to, Oh my goodness. Serious. Um-hmm. How was he to endure that? So he asked, "What all do you paint?"

"Not houses."

He grinned down at her. If she could be that sassy and knowing, she might make it with him...even if she did paint pictures.

"You got a...portfolio?" And he sweat just a little in fumbling for the word. He wanted to sound like he knew what she did.

She only nodded and didn't go into detailing what exactly she did in the Arts. She looked at his naked face. He was earnest. He was vulnerable. She needed to be careful of him. Her mouth said, "You'd be a marvelous painting...with that background." She indicated the out and beyond, past the oaks.

He gasped, "Naked?"

She tilted her head thoughtfully and considered.

Then she replied, "You could be. The bare land and a bare man. It would be more interesting to paint the background as bleak and you as a cowboy. People love cowboys."

"You?"

How was she to reply? She tilted her head again in thought and she told him, "You are perfect as a cowboy. It's rather shocking that you ride in a plane instead of on a horse."

"We ain't got no flying horses on this here place."

She laughed, clapped her hands and said, "That's the first time you've allowed your tongue to actually say those kinds of words. Do you do that often? Or do you just wait for the Yankee, winter snowbirds?"

"We do our best for them, ma'am. It is a *trial* that we endure, winters, to garner them there Yankee dollars—which is authentic, legal tender."

She nodded as she bit her lower lip to stop her laugh. "If I recall, the Confederate money is the questionable one, but the Yankees have always thought their money was good."

"You all got any of that there Confederate money?"

"We do." Her voice became soft. "It's been split among the family members so many times, in these last more than a hundred thirty years, that we don't have all that we once did. What we have is precious."

With some curiosity, she asked, "What would you write about Andrew's accident?"

Rip didn't even hesitate. "He was out where he shouldn't have been, on private land without permission."

"His viewpoint would be different."

Rip muttered, "He's a pilgrim."

Lu nodded gently as she looked slowly around. "He's a nuisance."

"There might be hope for you."

"Mother and I are stable people."

So, of course, he inquired, "You stable people like horses?"

Lu sighed as she softly told the wind, "Good gravy."

So Rip exclaimed, "What's *gravy* got to do with horses?"

"I believe you've been too far out and alone too much." She gestured. "You need to be in touch—"

He kissed her. He took her against his hungry body, and he groaned as his steely arms crushed her to him. Then he really kissed her. He held her head in one big hand so that the pressure of his kiss didn't break her neck.

He boggled her. When he gently released her, she had trouble standing up alone; she was not reliable. She put her hand on his chest and steadied herself. She didn't even notice how sparked he was. His eyes were wide and serious. His breathing was broken.

She wobbled. At least he could stand up. She had to keep her hand on his chest to steady herself. And her hand felt the wild beating of his heart. She looked at him and frowned because she couldn't focus her eyes.

Her soft red lips managed to communicate, "You dirty rat." Her eyelids were so heavy that she had to tilt up her chin in order to see him over her cheekbones.

Instantly, with his squint wrinkles pale, his face was serious as he asked, "You like rats?"

She breathed, her hand still on his chest to keep her reasonably stable as she elaborated, "You're—dangerous."

Earnestly, he told her, "I'm careful. I wouldn't hurt you for all the world."

His words triggered her. "This world is the only inhabitable one we can find. The astronauts have found that out. This fragile, overpopulated world is the only one we have."

So he asked, "Did you watch *Star Trek* on TV? They found all kinds of worlds."

She mumbled, "Fiction."

He gently tugged her against him and hugged her to his hungry body. "You're coming around. I'll make up a list of comments that'll stir your mind after I've blanked you out by kissing you."

Her puffed lips managed, "You are wicked."

He laughed unfairly in his throat like men know how to do. He said, "You kissed me back."

"How shocking!"

He loved it. She didn't deny her involvement. She admitted it. How was he going to keep this woman? Why her? She was so fragile. Could she endure sharing his life clear out there? He loved what he did. How could he trap such a woman, out there, on the edge of forever?

If she should stay with him, Rip knew her days out there would be lonely. He considered Lu and decided he'd be more careful of her. He had to give her room. She had to know what it would be like if they were to survive together.

Why was he thinking she would *want* to stay with him? Why would a woman like her want to tie up with a guy like him? And he couldn't think of any real reason, except sex. If that was his only lure to her, how long would the lure last?

The thought came, if Tom Keeper was around at all, she'd just switch over to him.

And Rip's feeling of self-worth diminished.

That's always bad for a man. Especially a flyer. He was silent. He didn't see how long it took her to recover from his kiss. He was aware that the reason she had put her hand on his chest was in order to stabilize herself. She was deliberately touching him. If she didn't like him, she could easily avoid touching him. He didn't see that. He saw only his flaws. Men are sometimes that way. They can be very irritatingly stupid.

They went back to Rip's little house. She thought it was charming. She smiled at it. She went up the steps to the open porch and sat on one of the rocking chairs. It rocked just exactly right.

Silent, Rip sat on the other rocking chair. He didn't tell her that he'd gotten them from the storage barn that held a fascinating accumulation of all sorts of things.

He'd washed the chairs carefully. He'd known Lu would like a rocking chair. He'd been right.

She said, "This is perfect. You're not on a street to look at the other houses so you get to look out and beyond. It's lovely."

He said, "So are you." Then he bit into his lower lip for his mouth being so pushy.

She laughed softly. "I like a prejudiced man."

He told her rather earnestly, "It wasn't prejudice. It's the truth. How can I ever impress you?"

"You saved my brother."

"Buddy did that. I don't know how your airhe— How your brother got such a good dog to take care of him."

"Airhead pretty much identifies Andrew. He is not of this world. He's off on a circle that doesn't include any of the current population on this earth. He is very like our father."

"You warning me off?"

"You need to know."

"I know." He was telling her that he understood the whole shebang, and he was willing to cope.

She cautioned, "It could be genetic."

"I have an uncle who collects seashells and he has boxes of them in his attic."

Her eyes sparkled. "Glory be."

"Well, he can't hold a candle to your brother, but he is a little odd."

Her eyes sparkled with laughter but she only bit her lower lip and then licked it gently. She was so amused. That he would share his uncle's overcollection of shells to match her brother's odd behavior was really very tender.

Sitting on the porch, in the breeze, was so relaxing. The couple talked and gestured and looked at each other. They laughed with such ease. He told her of the things he did while flying, what he looked for and how. He told her of his radio talks with people he knew only through talking, but he'd become known to them.

He indicated that he was a good flyer.

That was redundant to her. He'd be alert and interested in anything he did. His attention wouldn't be casually distracted.

The cellular phone rang, and it was Tom Keeper. He told Rip, "I see you got company. Want to bring her up for supper? We'd like another voice in our arguments."

Rip had already known he was welcome to sit at the table. It was a courtesy to be sure they included Rip's guest. He said, "I'd be obliged."

Tom cautioned, "Don't bring that dog. He'd have my bed the first night!"

That made Rip laugh. "Yeah. It's true. I'll feed him here and let him guard the place."

"I do appreciate that." Tom's voice was light and full of laughter. Tom already knew how Andrew Parsons's damned dog was a pusher in all sorts of sly ways.

But... Ahhh. Rip knew there was always a *but* that went with just about anything. If they did go to the big house for supper, and they would, Tom Keeper would again get to look at Lu Parsons. Tom was a capital Somebody, and he was a man who was anxious to find a woman of his own. He was good-looking and a man of means.

Rip looked over at Lu. She was perfect. Any woman would prefer a monied man who had the time to play and travel. It was just as well that he allow Tom to try for Lu. If Tom could lure Lu away from

Rip… Could he? And Rip's eyes flinched because he knew the answer to that one.

It was about five-thirty when Rip gave Lu a comb and watched her comb her hair and tidy herself. With his hands in his trouser pockets, he stood in the doorway of the bedroom where there was a mirror for her to see herself. She had worn a dress just in case they would have gone somewhere to eat that noon.

But it was evening. Now they would go to the main house. Her gown was a day dress. She was somewhat interested in how formal the Keepers would be. She was dressed as she was, and invited, and she would just see what their reactions would be.

And she would meet them all.

As Rip took her up to the big house for supper, he asked her, "Got any news to share at the table?"

She considered with a tilting of her head. "These are the Wide Open Spaces everybody thinks is TEXAS."

His eyes laughed. "Being an Easterner must be a heavy burden. But at least you say TEXAS in caps."

Biting a grin, her eyes dancing, she asked, "How'd you know that?"

"The senior Mrs. Keeper had me in the little room for lunch and manners for quite some time, and we discussed many things."

"She fell in love with you, but was committed to her family and couldn't run away with you."

His eye wrinkles bare, he said softly, "Hold that thought."

"That the senior Mrs. Keeper fell in love with you? She did?"

His voice low, he explained very carefully, "That a woman could love me."

She laughed. "You silly." She shook her head. "You probably have a little black book with all sorts of names and phone numbers of women who insist you want them. How do you manage all those women?"

"I'm only interested in one. You."

Her flushed face turned pale and her mouth opened so that her lungs had an outlet and could drag in some oxygen…as soon as her brain cleared and she remembered how to do that. She said, "Oh."

Well, that was better than silence. But Rip was riveted by the fact that he could boggle her.

It was then in silence that they went to the main house. Lu met all the people there. And they were charming.

There are just some people with élan, and the Keepers were such people. They were casually dressed. Tom was only one of several Keeper offspring.

The table was nicely set, and quite a few people were there who did not live on the compound.

Everyone knew one another except for Lu, and she was nicely introduced so that she understood who was attached to whom and how.

Tom Keeper looked at Lu with serious eyes. He'd seen her at the hospital, but he obviously had not caught her attention. Tom smiled at Rip and moved his head in a way that said, *How'd you get her so quick?*

But Rip wasn't amused. He was deadly serious and, with one hand on Lu, he indicated that she was solely his.

Rip never really let go of her. Tom understood. Lu didn't mind at all.

She knew of the Keepers. Everybody who was anybody already knew of them. So did Lu. Mrs. Keeper said, "I know your mama. She is a wonderful woman."

Lu smiled. "She's a strict, hard-nosed, riveting starer who, on some occasions, will smile."

Mrs. Keeper laughed as she said, "My mama is exactly that same way!"

Lu gasped, "Still?"

Mrs. Keeper nodded. "She's never let up even for five minutes. But I'm on to her now, since my kids are grown, I tolerate her and even decline sharing some private things."

Lu urged with intense interest, "How soon can I try that angle with my mama?"

Mrs. Keeper suggested, "In ten years?"

With faked dismay, Lu tsked and added, "Not 'til then?"

"If she's at all like *my* mama, she'll never let up, but I do believe your mama is more tolerant. I have a cousin who knows her, and she loves your mama."

"I do, too," Lu agreed. But being the age she was, she added, "—from a distance."

While it seemed as if Mrs. Keeper would be the one who really controlled the table and the people,

Lu had already heard about Mr. Keeper. He looked so easy, but Lu had heard how he could be.

It was a rare time that it was Mr. Keeper who markedly changed a subject. There had been times, between courses, that it was Mr. Keeper who invited a thorn out to see his new horse. On rarer occasions, the thorn didn't return with Mr. Keeper...the guest was excused from the company by Mr. Keeper as "...been called away." Once it had been a woman.

That night, at the table, it was a surprise when some male mentioned he had to leave because he was flying in the morning. The person saying that then almost smiled at Rip.

Rip nodded once with some gentle recognition.

The other guy was George, and he was volunteering to take Rip's flight in the morning. George was a smart cookie. Now Rip would owe him one. George stood and almost ducked his head to his hostess who told him to fly low and slow.

That was *always* said.

And Mr. Keeper stood and said, "Thank you," to George.

That sounded very like Mr. Keeper knew George was doing something special, but Mr. K. always did that to anybody on the ranch who helped. Besides good wages, the Keepers gave out a lot of thank-yous.

It was after eleven before the dinner party actually broke up. They'd been talking and arguing and laughing all that time. There were fewer of them since so many of the workers had early hours, but it had been a stimulating, laughing time, and Lu had enjoyed it all.

After their farewells and thanks to their hosts, Lu and Rip walked over to his house. He said kindly to her, "You're just lucky I have an extra bedroom and you don't have to go back to town tonight."

"Could I borrow your pickup and go to the hospice?"

"You *sure* you need to go all-the-way back to town? It's late."

"Go to bed. I'm stimulated enough to stay awake for the drive. And I can drive your pickup okay. You can trust me to be careful."

"I think Willie said that same thing to me before he totaled my last pickup. The words have a familiar ring."

"He...died?"

Rip shook his head. "Willie was too drunk to be harmed. He was sleeping in the crumpled mess when the ambulance came to him."

"How'd they know to look for him?"

Rip shrugged. "Somebody saw the wreck and the lax body inside it all, and they called in."

"Willie was dumb."

Rip went on to explain, "He's on the wagon. Off it, and he gets to leave here for good."

"Good."

Rip sighed with great forbearance. "I'm gonna have to take you home? It's such a long way, and you could sleep over, here, and I could take you back tomorrow."

"If I stayed here, my mother would have kittens."

In a very fake astonishment, Rip exclaimed, "Your sweet mama's a *cat?*"

"Of course." And she hissed at him as she curled her fingers. It was a lousy try.

He suggested, "Practice that a little more."

So she thoughtfully hissed and considered her tries. She curled her fingers and observed that. She gave it up. "I didn't get the right genes."

"You're a woman."

"I'd noticed."

"—you could sleep with me."

"Not this time."

He gasped and stopped and breathed.

She frowned at him in the street-lighted dark so he saw what she was doing and anyway, he had remarkable vision as a licensed flyer. She asked, "Are you all right?"

"Right? Half of me is left."

She faked it: "Har, har, har."

He expanded it, "You really steam me. Let me love you."

"Not yet."

Now, that was a really nasty thing to do to a man as chancy as Rip was at that time. He breathed rather strangely.

She frowned at him and used her fingers to turn his face to one of the light posts strung along the road. "What's the matter with you?"

And he replied in a husky voice, "You."

She said, "Oh, for crying out loud. Behave."

"Well, help me. You keep saying things and walking thataway and breathing. What all do you expect of me?" His tone was indignant.

Knowing full well he would object, she said, "I'll hitchhike."

He sighed with great tolerance and quite a lot of drama. He said, "I'm going to have to *drive* you all the way to the hospice so that your parents can know you're there…safely."

Her parents were on the other side of the state and assumed she could take care of herself. But she said, "Yes."

He turned her face gently so that the light pole showed him what she looked like. He groused, "By George, you really *do* look like an angel. How come you don't *act* like one?"

"I am." She licked her lips and allowed a small smile on her face as she looked up at him. "I'm being pure."

And he said, "Well, hell."

Six

So that night, that late, Rip drove for an hour down the two-lane highway, to get Lu back to the hospice. It was the most interesting time because they both talked all the way. They weren't animated or quarreling or debating, they just exchanged ideas and comments.

However, when they got to the silent streets where the hospital hospice was, Rip drove carefully and he looked around. The streets were lighted. The town no longer had any problem with nighthawks. That's what they'd called those ones who once had swooped around like "birds of prey."

As Rip stopped the pickup, he pushed back the seat and reached for Lu, preventing her escape.

She cautioned him in a very soft voice, "This isn't wise."

His voice was foggy. He told her very quickly in an earnest manner, "It'll keep me awake all the way back to the ranch."

She began saying, "You're limited to—" But he never knew.

He kissed her until her brain smoothed out and she had no resistance at all. Men are clever that way.

But, eventually, the night patrol tapped on the windshield with her flashlight. The tapping finally was identified to Rip's brain as not being his racketing heart but something else. He lifted his hungry mouth from Lu's, but he didn't ease his intense arms as he looked fuzzily out of the windshield.

Through the windshield, the woman told Rip, "Your time here is overparked."

Obviously, the woman was tactful. Rip nodded. Then with Herculean effort, he commanded his arms and hands to withdraw from the female draped bonelessly across his chest.

He told Lu, "It's time for you to go inside. I'll walk you to the door."

With closed eyes, and a totally lax body, she struggled with the effort in making the words clear. Her puffed lips asked slowly, slowly, "Do…you… have…a…condom?"

That just about ruined him for good. Good? Well…forever. He practiced breathing for a time and his body was berserker. He shivered. His mind told his body he was in control. That hilarity was enjoyed by all his rioting cells. That included even most of his brain!

Since his body was in such a state, Rip figured he actually did have a guardian angel just like his grandmother had told him, long ago. That was sobering. He'd ignored the guardian for most of his life. Was the guardian the one who'd saved his neck all those times when he'd been recklessly sure of landing or avoiding or flying close and looking?

He'd thought he relied on his own skills. It was a dot demeaning to think Somebody else was in charge of him. How bored that— Well, actually, his guardian had been fortunate to've had Rip to be with and experience all Rip had shared—however unknowingly.

In his mind, he said, *Okay. This time. Now get out of here!*

He opened his pickup's door and slid out from under Lu. Then he propped her on the seat so that he could close his door and he went around the truck so that he could open her door.

He had to help the gelatin-mass in getting out of the truck. He did that kindly and with a whole lot of satisfaction that he'd affected her so completely. In all her life, she would never forget him. She would line up any other man's skills alongside what she'd had from Rip Morris. His knowledge of his effect on her was a grim victory of defeat.

So, at the front door of the hospice, Rip took about fifteen minutes to kiss the soft-mouthed, heavily breathing, pawing woman good-night. He was so rigid he couldn't bend. But he was being unfair with her, and he knew it. She was a shambles. He smiled with some regret. This was goodbye.

But things don't always happen the way a man thinks they will go. Early the next morning, when Rip took Buddy into town to see Andrew at the hospital, there she was.

What other "she" was there? He gave up all those earnest commitments he'd acknowledged to leaving her be. He discarded the fact they were not suited...in practical ways. They were worlds apart.

She blushed as she smiled softly.

That just about ruined Rip. He stared at her with naked eyes. He asked softly, "Is he asleep?"

She nodded, blushing deeper.

But Buddy went over to the other side of the bed and stretched up to put his front paws on the bed so that he was about face-to-face with Andrew. And in his throat, the dog said a whole lot of things about what all had gone on between those two who were on the other side of the bed.

Buddy blabbed *everything*—right off—and had no qualms about any of it. There was no question, at all, that was what the dog was doing, without a doubt. The blasted dog was a *gossip!*

At least Andrew was asleep— But then Andrew coughed in a strangled manner.

The two potential lovers frowned at the back of Andrew's head. Even if he was awake, he couldn't *possibly* understand all the gossip that was flowing out of that damned dog's mouth.

Rip growled quietly to Lu, "That dog is as mouthy as a wet-eared...kid." He'd changed the word at the last minute because he realized if he actually said "woman" Lu might be ticked.

Instead, she gently soothed him, "The dog is just making noises, trying to communicate."

Without any confidence in that reply, Rip limited himself to a nothing, "Yeah."

Rip watched her. Her eyelashes closed down over her eyes as she blushed for some reason. Why was she acting shy? What was it about him that made her blush? His clothes were tidy. He looked. She wasn't embarrassed. She hadn't done or said anything that would cause her to become shy.

So Rip asked, "What's the matter?"

And with lazy eyes, she readily replied, "You haven't kissed me."

That was like a lightning bolt right through his body and caught in his sex. And since the bolt first went through his throat, he couldn't get his vocal cords to work at all. He just concentrated on standing, watching his feet shift as he tried seriously to breathe.

Women were a nuisance.

Men can hardly make it without one.

Life is strange.

Rip was wondering if he could take her quietly out to the ranch that morning. While that was an intense thought, he knew it would never work. The problem with it was that people would see she was there. As empty as the roads were and the land around the house, *some* nosy-minded body would look out a window and see that Rip had a woman with him.

The word would spread through the whole area in less than five minutes. The only reason it would take that long is that people chatter and a man can't just give news but has to listen, too!

Rip looked at Lu very seriously. She was so innocent. She probably had no idea how they could be together and not be seen. He was stymied. How could he ever find a way to get her?

And he remembered the proprietors of that place, Marge and Hank! YES! They *expected* him to sleep with that woman! Why not?

He smiled at the idea that he was going to get her into a real bed and without the dog. She could have the opportunity to cure him so that he could again think and move and be himself.

No woman ever realized the torture she put a man through.

He watched her. Those fake eyelashes were really something. They were so black on that blond woman. She must carry a ton of mascara with her to always have her lashes so black. Her eyebrows were just sorta brown.

He wondered if she bleached her hair. He'd find out when he stripped her bare. And he groaned at the very thought of her stripping...for him or just by herself. How could she be so selfish as to strip that body raw when he couldn't be there to see her do it?

He needed something else to think about. He said, "Wanna play poker?"

And she wickedly replied, "Okay. Strip."

His eyes went vulnerable. His mouth opened with his silent gasp of shock. He said, "Why, Lu, you're wicked!" And he put his hand on his chest as if he was an innocent with no such thoughts.

But Lu corrected him. "I am so curious! You'd be the perfect teacher. I'll soon be back home, and I ought to have something by which I can remember this unusual, rather isolated, primitive place. You're it. Fortunately, we don't know each other well enough for me to harm you in any way. It'll be a chance encounter. I'll remember you all of my life, as my first."

Very seriously and in some shock, Rip inquired, "I'll just be your—first? Now just how many innocent men have you planned on having?"

And her reply sobered him considerably more. She said, "I'll see."

That certainly did make Rip frown. But he wasn't about to scold her. If she was willing, that was something he needed to encourage. And his need went through his body in a thrilling wave. He was going to get her.

Temporarily.

His mind saw the word TEMPORARILY in blinking lights, and he was sobered. It was like he was standing on the edge of a cliff top and the ground was giving out under his feet. He felt like scrambling. But he didn't know what way to go.

Well, he did know that. She was right over there. He found that his legs would move, so his feet went over to her and the rest of him went along. Since her brother was silent and facing the other way, Rip lifted the wicked woman into his arms, against his urgent body, and he gave her his killer kiss.

His brain dissolved, his hands turned to steel, and so did his sex. His breathing labored. How was he to cope with such a blunder?

As she kissed him back, the dog barked once.

Since the dog had warned him, Rip had released Lu, stabilized her fluid body somewhat, and put his hands into his pant pockets.

The sassy redheaded nurse came into the room and said to Andrew, "It's time to wake up and let me move you around some more." She then grinned at the comatose couple who were locked in some time lapse, stiffened and dead-faced.

Ignoring the two, the nurse moved Andrew around and grunted and gasped doing it so that he had to help her. Women can be very sly. Men can, too. But women get help they don't always need by being so frail and gorgeous like the redheaded nurse.

Andrew said, "Ouch."

The nurse heartlessly exclaimed, "You have feeling in that leg! That's just great! Let's see if you can bend the knee."

She was mean! Anybody listening to Andrew would know that. That nurse probably stuck pins in flies.

And more than likely, she only said "yes" to a man when they were trapped in a large, noisy crowd where she knew she was perfectly safe!

Lu noticed him watching the nurse, and cooled. Yep. Any man knows a woman always cools off for any sort of stupid excuse. Just having another woman in the same room had frosted Lu. Now just when would he ever be able to get Lu back on track and willing? Who could ever know? Women were very odd for an earnest man.

So being the age he was, he told the dog to come along and they'd leave the patient to cope with the nurse alone. Then he asked Lu, "Want to come along and have a cup of coffee...on me?"

She looked at him thoughtfully as if to consider if he was really human or just a portion of his body was that. Her eyes then slid over to the redheaded nurse and she told Rip, "All right."

Rip's eyes squinched as he considered her reply. It was better than nothing, but for some reason, God only knew why, she was ticked off at him. He wondered what he'd done for her to react thataway.

Although the door was open, Rip put his hand on the knob as if he was holding it for her, then he followed her out into the hall. The two almost-lovers went down the hall toward the elevator.

Just then, they came upon a little old, bent-over lady. She was chewing her gums and seemed determined to creep along the hallway, holding on to the nurse and an endless, chest-high bar. The helper with her was speaking loudly and talking to the woman as if she was a child.

The old woman's amused eyes touched and lingered on Rip to share the humor.

But when Rip laughed in his chest and swallowed the sound, Lu asked with indignation, "What's so funny?"

"That helper is treating the little old lady like she's senile."

Lu replied, "She probably is."

"Well, if she is, then there's still her humor that is bubbling up at this time. She was amused by the helper hollering at her."

But Lu suggested, "Maybe she was laughing at you."

Knowing full well that he was a well set-up male, and no logical victim of humor, Rip retreated a tad. He replied, "Ummm."

Something like that is very irritating to any woman who is ready to quarrel.

As they walked along, Lu began to assess herself and her attempt at a quarrel with Rip just because that redheaded nurse had come into Andrew's room. She was jealous of the nurse, who was cheerful, helpful, and sly at getting the useless patient to do as she said.

The nurse was able to accomplish that. Lu had never been able to put a bend in any part of her brother Andrew's thinking in all her born days. Lu was jealous. The nurse just did as she was directed by the doctors. Lu owed an apology to Rip for her conduct.

So she looked up at his face, and as his eyes turned to her, she smiled. Then she looked away, having done all she needed to do.

But Rip frowned, his steps lagged because he was trying to understand what Lu's smile meant. Women are so interesting and alluring, but serious men never knew which way to go with one. Of course, selfish men were never bothered with understanding a woman.

Since it was visiting hours and they passed Chuck's room, they stopped and the dog went in to the boy and put his forepaws on the side of the bed. Then as the boy smoothed the dog's head, he talked to the dog in a natural voice and told him, "I'm so glad to see you. Are you laughing at me? Or is that the way you say hello? I have a dog that doesn't laugh at all. He will go along and he'll watch, but he doesn't tell me anything like you do. I'm glad you came by."

The dog's throat made all those sounds that people

never understand, but the boy nodded and appeared to listen.

Lu wondered what all the dog was telling, and then she watched the boy to see if he understood the sounds.

The bedfast boy appeared to just watch the dog, but smart grown-ups never trust earnest children. Such kids are mentally beyond their age and they are skilled in keeping secrets. They accept confidences from dogs. Then Lu wondered if, in all her days, she'd ever understood a dog or if she'd ever tried. She had not.

As the two humans sat at one of the cafeteria's outside tables, where the dog was allowed, Lu looked around. She was waiting for Rip to smooth things out and be especially darling to her.

He was silent.

There is just nothing more irritating than an adult male who waits for a woman to settle down and make some effort in trying to be reasonably adult. Men are seldom any help at a time like this. How irritating. She gave him a scathing look and found he wasn't looking at her, he was considering his plate.

And she was startled.

He was looking at his plate with just about the same hunger that he looked at her!

Men are so basic. Food and women. Probably in that order. With some men, a woman came first. Men have almost starved wanting an indifferent woman. It was true. Lu looked at Rip as he relished his food. He wouldn't pine for any woman. There'd be another just down the pike.

But for the usual man, next to food there would be his interest in a woman. Well, there would be another interest that would have to include money. Yeah. And, of course, baseball. *And* football. The races. Magazines with naked women. That sort of thing.

Yep. Lu sighed without seeming to. But men are all women have. It was rather dispiriting to realize there is no alternative.

Rip looked over at Lu and saw that she was considering her plate. That proved she had her appetite back and would eat. He'd worried about her eating. Even at the Keepers' Place while Lu was listening and laughing, she hadn't eaten very much. Along with being in a strange place with strange people, she worried about her useless brother.

Lu carefully took up a quarter sandwich and bit into it with hesitation. Rip admired her gentleness. He'd once, in Houston, had a woman stevedore who had boggled him, she was so different. With both elbows on the table, she'd eaten from a full sandwich held by both hands. She'd been an experience.

He'd run from her like a puppy with his tail between his legs.

Lu asked, "When can we be…together?"

He almost choked. That was probably good because with trying to breathe, he was a tiny bit distracted from what she'd actually said to him. He looked at her.

It would have interested him how he'd exposed that fragile skin around his eyes just because of this woman, right there, in front of him. With the TEXAS sun, he'd squinted all his born days! He was so used to squinting that he even did that when he wore the colored sunglasses. That skin, alongside his eyes, was fragile…and she was causing him to expose that tender skin to the wicked elements. One way and another, she was ruining him.

And just now, she'd asked him when they could be together! Now, how was a man to handle that? Say…"huh?" Or "who wants to know?" Or "shame on you?" So with those naked eyes, he asked, "Now?"

She tilted her head to one side and raised her eyebrows as she replied, "After we've eaten."

Who wanted food! His sex was on overdrive and the roots of his desire had expanded until there was no room in his body for food. He put down the sandwich and just said logically, while the iron was still hot. "Let's go."

She asked, "Where?"

"I'll find a place."

So being the kind of woman she was, she wrapped the sandwiches in paper napkins and rose.

He had a little more trouble getting up…from the chair…there. But he had reached over and put a hand under her arm so that she could lift her precious, fragile body from the chair.

He paid for their lunch and took her elbow carefully so that she didn't trip on a discarded toothpick or something dangerous like that.

He put her into the cab of his pickup and went around to get into the driver's seat. Then he drove around, looking, and saw a drugstore. He parked two blocks away.

She asked logically, "Where are you going?"

And he replied pithily, "I need—something from

the drugstore.'' He looked at her seriously to communicate with her.

But she was looking around and then moved her hand to indicate the street as she said, ''There're parking places up by that drugstore down the way.''

He was very tender. ''I don't want anybody seeing me coming out to the pickup with you in it.''

''You're ashamed of...me?''

''Naw. You're a fragile lady and I don't want anybody gossiping about you.''

She looked at him blankly, but he thought she was admiring him, so he walked on off with something of a strut. He stopped a couple of times to let people go on by him, and he finally went into the drugstore.

It took him forever. He browsed and selected and casually neglected to include condoms...from a fake list he pretended to follow.

He told the checkout girl, ''Boy, you go into town for something and *every*body wants something for themselves.'' He went over the blank paper, hunched over. Then he said, ''I forgot Paul's.'' So he went back for condoms.

The checkout girl made no comment at all. She was simply bored and busy.

When Rip eventually got back to the pickup, and deposited that big sack behind his seat, Lu was really quite ticked.

He got into the driver's seat and buckled his seat belt as he said with satisfaction, ''Got some.''

That seemed too odd. She inquired with a frown, ''Did you get the...protection? What all did you buy, for crying out loud?''

He was logical, ''I couldn't just go into the store

and get condoms. *Everybody* in the *area* would know!'' He was quite pleased with himself. ''So I pretended I had a list from a whole lot of others,'' he bragged in a very nice way. Then he went on, ''And I went back for the condoms when I was checking the list!'' He was smug because he'd been so clever.

She was jolted. But he was turning around in mid-block and going the other way!

She asked logically, ''Where are we going?'' If they were going back the way they'd come, the lone, two-lane road into town had had only ranch branch-offs.

Very seriously, he told her, ''I'm gonna go over to another street to get out of town so's nobody will suspect what I'm going to do with you.''

That seemed so crass. So... *Underhanded* wasn't exactly the word she wanted at that time. A virgin, she already felt like a ruined woman.

So silently they drove out of the little town and on down the gentle swells of occasional ripples in the tableland. There were cotton fields and wheat fields and telephone poles and fences and not much else. Well, there were mesquites.

Lu considered how she was committing herself to be with Rip in this experiment. And she decided why not? She needed to be a little friendlier. If she was to do this, he should take pleasure in it, too. She didn't want to just use him. They should share.

She told Rip, ''You're very special.''

He laughed.

That rather surprised Lu. She wasn't sure what to say next. But it was obvious that if she was going to do this reckless thing, she ought to be a bit more friendly and open with him.

So she said in a breathless way with naked eyes, "This is exciting."

Rip's eyes sparkled with his humor. He replied, "Yeah."

Ahead, there was a turnoff.

He grinned. "I knew this was here! We got a place!"

That shivered Lu considerably. Her eyes were sober. She stretched her mouth into a smile because she felt she should seem to be interested. If she was going to have such an experience, this was the time to do it, while she was clear across the whole expanse of TEXAS, just about, and at such a crossroads that no one would *ever* hear anything at all about her conduct in that place.

At least not from Mrs. Keeper.

He told Lu, "As I recall, there's a turnoff to a dump place in a couple of miles. We'll go there."

She was shocked. Her first thrilling sexual encounter—in a dump? How basic. All they'd remember would be the smell from the dump. She could be ruined for all the rest of her sexual life! He probably wouldn't notice any smell. He'd probably think it was she. In the years ahead, he'd probably say with some nostalgia, "I once had a real ripe woman."

The road wound on down into a mild gully, and there was the turnoff...and there by the side of the road, was a car with a man under a raised car hood.

Yeah.

Inside the car was a woman and two very small children.

Rip didn't say anything but just stopped the pickup. Then he said to Lu, "I'll be a minute or so." He got out of the pickup and took out his tool chest from behind the seat. He walked over and asked, "What's wrong?" And the two men's heads disappeared under the hood of the car.

So Lu got out and went over to the car and told the woman, "Would you like to come sit in the pickup? The air conditioner is on."

And the woman said, "Thanks. Come on, kids."

In Rip's pickup, Lu sat under the steering wheel to protect the car's fascinating ignition keys and pedals. Back east, she had small cousins who were dangerous in cars. Being able to know something like that was probably why it was important for people to have relatives.

The woman said nothing. The kids screeched and fought and were everywhere. The mother was probably on some drug the doctor gave her so she didn't have to cope with the kids. She was in La La Land?

So since it was her vehicle, well, it was Rip's, Lu flipped over, knelt on the seat and reached over into the limited back seat to separate the two quarreling kids. Through her teeth, she said, "Be quiet!"

They snarled at her and almost hit her, but she was used to such little beasts and said in a dire voice, "One more time of such sass, and you're out of the air-conditioning and tied on a short rope."

She had no rope. It was an empty threat.

The woman stayed silent.

Then Lu said, "I shall tell you a story." It was said in a deadly manner with squinched eyes that were threatening.

She told them the story about the little boy who turned into a jackass and could only bray. He just about starved because he couldn't speak and ask for food. He grew big long ears and his mouth humped over and his teeth grew.

The kids listened.

And she finished the story with, "A child must be careful and pleasant in this world. If he is not careful, he could run into just such a magic person who is offended by the behavior of rude children."

One asinine child said, "The magic guy weren't so nice. Look what he done."

And she asked, "Why did he do it?"

"I don' know."

So she explained. "Because the nasty child wasn't polite and he annoyed a magic person who didn't spank him. He just turned the nasty child into a donkey and the child couldn't use words again."

The other kid said, "I don' believe it."

And Lu replied, "Neither did he."

With that odd reply, she could be saying the story was fake or the boy was stupid.

So then Lu told the story about the Little Engine That Could.

Being an aunt sometimes comes in handy. But the looks Lu gave the silent mother were not kind. The woman turned her face to the car window and was withdrawn.

Although it seemed an interminable time, it wasn't more than a half hour, or so, before there was the sound of an engine roaring across the road.

The kids yelled with it. Then they said to Lu. "Finish."

Mannerly children.

Lu opened the door and dragged out the two child beasts as she said in a kind voice, "Go to the library and ask for the book."

The woman got out on the other side of the car. As she passed Lu she said, "Thanks, honey," and she trudged off across the empty highway without watching for the kids at all.

Lu dragged the kids back and said, "Look first left, then right, then left again before you cross a street." She snatched them back about three or four times until they did as she said. Then the two small beasts crossed the street, turned back and thumbed their noses at her.

Seven

Having wiped his hands on a cloth from his tool chest, Rip walked back to his pickup on the other side of the two-lane, endless road. He put his bag of tools behind the seat then got into the pickup. He said to Lu, "That was nice of you to take that woman into the pickup. Thank you. I wasn't sure you'd want her along."

"Why not?"

"She's a loose woman." Rip was honest. "Pack had the kids today, and he got her for a while. The kids are little enough not to notice."

"Ahhhh," Lu ah-ed, "So that's why she didn't have any control over those little beasts."

"They appeared to be listening to you." Rip was impressed. "What all did you say to them?"

Direly she retorted, "I made them settle down, and

I told them some pithy stories about behavior. They are out of control!''

"I saw you show them how to cross a road. That was very nice of you."

Thoughtfully, she considered, "I'm not sure they should survive."

Rip laughed in genuine humor.

She did not.

As they drove along, Rip was saying rather regretfully, "I guess it was a good thing Pack was stopped there."

Apparently, he thought that was enough for Lu to realize. But she asked, "Why?"

"I'd forgotten this is dump week. Whoever's turn it is to cover the trash, does the monthly tractor covering next week."

She was droll. "That must be exciting."

"Naw. It's boring. My turn is a while coming, since we have such a bunch at the ranch. But if you and I had been in this pickup along the highway anywhere around here, we might have been surprised by a lot of people coming past on their way to the dump—and honking at us."

She sighed. "I suppose it's hopeless. You can't even come inside the hospice."

He soothed her, "I'll find us a way."

She didn't see how he'd be able to do that and was silent. Then she said, "With all this room, out here in West TEXAS, it shouldn't be that difficult for us to be alone."

Rip nodded. "It seems so, but people keep track of each other out here. It's like with Pack. He knew somebody would come along, but having that woman with him was a chancy thing as to who the rescuer would be. He was really glad to see me."

"Why?"

"I wouldn't mention the woman to anybody."

She responded in a rather hostile reminder, "I will."

Rip laughed softly as he inquired in a very kind manner, "What's her name?"

"I need to know?"

He assured her. "Not at all. You thought that woman was Pack's wife. You have no idea who she is. And you don't know the name of his wife. You don't live around here, so you won't ask. The woman wasn't chatting with you, at all, I watched."

Lu asked, "Do you know who she is?"

"Nope. I didn't ask."

Lu commented, "I wonder if his wife knows."

"If you ever meet her, don't ask her."

Lu was disgusted. "I wouldn't."

"And don't say—" His voice changed into the sound of what men think is a woman's tone, "'Oh, you do look so different.'"

Lu slid her eyes over toward him in a very tolerantly patient manner.

His eyes were filled with humor.

She was silent for a while before she mentioned softly. "We haven't found a place...to be."

His voice was roughened with his emotion and was very kind. He told her, "We will."

But it appeared to be just about impossible.

Then Rip had to go on a flight checkup that would take twenty-four hours. It would be overnight. Now, in that expanse of people at the place, any nonresident would think there'd be someone, out there, who would take in Andrew's dog. Right? Naw.

To Lu, Rip reasoned logically that whoever took care of the dog had to be somebody who knew Buddy and could keep the poor, almost totally abandoned dog stable. Rip had named Lu as the one to stay with her brother's dog.

So she asked, "Isn't there somebody out yonder, at your place, who can put food in his dish just twice in that twenty-four hours?"

Rip explained seriously, "He'd be lonesome."

"I'm to...baby-sit...a dog?"

Rip soothed, "It's a very widening experience. Doing something like that, you come to understand lonesome people. You become compassionate to a lonely flier who searches the skies and the land rifts for danger as he flies alone and isolated in a plane."

Her lazy voice was only on the other side of the car seat but it seemed to be softly in his very ear as Lu asked, "Now, how is my staying with the dog going to change your life, with you away all that time?"

Rip's voice was a little foggy. "I'll know you're in my bed."

She corrected that quite logically. "Oh, no. Not there. You'd have to change the sheets. I'll just sleep on the couch."

He was disgusted. "What a tacky thing to say! If you're going to sleep on the couch, don't mention it to me! I prefer to think of you as being in my bed. Don't louse me up thisaway. Anyway, it's your brother's dog. That alone would demand your attention. That dog walked his paws raw just to save your brother's neck.''

''Buddy should have saved Andrew's leg.''

Rip reminded her, ''Now you must know a dog that size couldn't move the horse.''

''I know.''

Rip pushed. ''You coming out and taking care of your brother's dog?'' How like a man to find some leverage for a woman to do as he wanted.

Lu mentioned, ''I'm not sure Buddy realizes he's a dog. He does try to communicate. He thinks of himself as more of an equal.''

With laughter in his voice, Rip replied, ''Some dogs are thataway.'' Then he inquired, ''Are you avoiding committing yourself to one spell of twenty-four hours to take care of Andrew's dog?''

She sighed. ''Welllll, okay.''

''I'll give you a map on how to get out here from town. Naw, I'll come in ahead of time and—''

Lu interrupted. ''It would be an adventure to drive myself out. I'll do that. Having a car there will give me a means of getting around.''

Rather too quickly, Rip blurted, ''When you get out there, don't go visit with the Keepers.''

Impatiently, Lu protested, ''I'll have to. They'll know I'm there and it would be rude of me not to say hello.''

Rip warned, ''Don't even touch Tom.''

She exclaimed, ''Now, *why* would I do *that?*''

In a deadly voice, Rip enunciated, ''He's a catch for a woman.''

She retorted, ''He's very nice, but I'm not interested in him. He's just a nice guy.''

Rip growled, "Keep that thought."

So she warned carefully, "Don't get serious about me. I'll be leaving here, soon now."

He didn't want to verbally arm-wrestle her. He cautioned carefully, "But in the time you're here, you will stay with me."

Rather impatiently, she agreed, "For that time, okay. The dog and I will be at your house. But don't get territorial. I'll be leaving here when Andrew is better."

Rip thought how selfish Andrew was, and said with some irony, "That'll take a while."

But Lu took Rip literally and replied softly, "He doesn't seem to be coming out of it at all well."

So Rip knew positively that Lu thought Andrew was mostly out of it. Andrew was in perfectly good health except for his leg. Rip didn't know if he should straighten out Lu's compassion for her selfish brother or leave it alone as it was, for Rip's own sake. If she knew what a fraud her brother was, she might leave too soon...for his own plot.

Rip said, "We'll see." That TEXAS reply covers all sorts of murky things. It's the do all/end all reply of careful parents, or of lovers who are nervous and unsure but who want everything to go their own way. In any bind, they are carefully vague as they delay whatever it is that's hanging for a decision.

In that way, no matter what the problem or pending decision or required choice, "We'll see" is a careful postponement.

Having arrived and parked and trudged to Andrew's room in the hospital, the two potential lovers sat in Lu's brother's room playing a hot game of poker. The dog was stretched up, by the side of the bed, and was talking to the patient and blabbing everything!

Ignoring the dog's blabbing, the two visitors played with intense attention to the cards. Their pennies, nickles and dimes switched ownership with satisfied Hahs! from the winner. They were both quite basically competitive.

Since Rip was especially so, it was a surprise that Lu didn't realize how Rip manipulated her. He took her out to lunch, at Marge and Hank's, and privately he talked to Hank.

Marge chatted with Lu somewhat away from the conversation between Rip and Hank. Hank was smiling and earnest as he nodded.

As they drove from the eatery, Lu inquired, "What did you say to Hank?"

"When was that?"

"You talked and he nodded."

Realizing she was on the track and he couldn't wiggle out of this one, Rip told her, "I asked if we could have that upstairs room next week."

She gasped. "You didn't!"

"I told them that you are too good a sister, that Andrew doesn't seem to be progressing at all well, and you're exhausted. You might need to rest there next week."

"That *wouldn't* fool *anybody!*"

He chided, "They are compassionate people, and they take me at my word."

She considered their use of the room. She had listened to his logic. Hesitantly, she asked, "They believe you?"

He was soberly logical. "Of course. Why wouldn't they?"

She mulled the premise over with narrowed eyes. "It sounds sneaky."

"Naw. The ranch is a long way off—"

She reminded Rip, "I stay in the hospice. It isn't far from the hospital. I have no need to sleep at someone's place."

He sighed with endurance and told her kindly, "Don't rock the boat."

It was odd for a TEXAS tableland man to say such a thing. Then one remembers how many of the TEXAS sons were beyond discipline by the parents and sent to sea under a hard-nosed captain long enough to get through that twenty-year-old age.

Lu knew that. She was a TEXAN. She had a brother who had been on a ship for a spell—about a year, if she recalled it all. Andrew. He'd been very difficult in a most courteous manner.

Men are odd.

So being familiar with such a discipline, with Rip's use of naval language, Lu figured Rip had been out in the Gulf on a boat for a while.

She was right.

She looked at him in another way.

He thought by her eye-slit observation that she was uncertain instead of simply curious. He figured that she was concerned about his twenty-four-hour flight. So he said, bravely, "I'll be okay."

She was so amused by him, and his plotting, that she just smiled sweetly and let it all ride.

After a pause that was long enough, Lu asked, "Why are you able to spend all this time away from the ranch?"

An interesting question for a woman that young. He replied, "I'm a pilot. We have odd hours. We have to have time between the exhausting flights." He looked at her with clear, honest eyes.

Then he told her the truth, reminding her, "I got the care of Andrew's dog because I got him, right away, from Tom Keeper. I took Buddy up in the plane to see if he could guide me to find what worried him. He watched and did see your brother first."

Rip added seriously, "Buddy sticks to me like pieces of cotton. It was easier for the dog to be with somebody he already knows, and he tolerates flying remarkably well."

She nodded in understanding. "So he could go with you, and I wouldn't have to dog-sit him?"

Earnestly, Rip told her, "That long, long twenty-four hours, of flying, is just too long for such a dog. It's just about too long for a man. It's a testing. I don't need to be flying at night and be distracted by a dog that needs a tree."

"I can see that."

"So, since Buddy is your *brother's* dog—" he tended to underline that quite obviously "—it's only logical that you be the one to take care of Buddy when I can't."

She nodded rather carelessly as if the whole discussion was redundant.

They went to dinner at the hospital and sat outside because of the dog.

So was Rip...strange. Actually, all his manipulating was run-of-the-mill male plotting. He sat next to Lu at the table, outside at the hospital, and he looked at her.

Rip wanted Lu in his bed and he used her brother's dog as a commitment. He did that smoothly. Logically.

With her brother in the hospital, Andrew's dog was really her responsibility. Rip was just giving the dog a little freedom. Freedom? In the pickup. In the hospital. Yeah. But Buddy wasn't in some cage at a vet's place.

Lu observed the dog with tolerance. He was just a companion. The dog didn't need to be talked to or petted. He really acted quite mature for a dog. There were times when Lu suspected the dog was amused. Something in his eyes—

Naw, Buddy was only just a dog.

Rip gave Lu all sorts of directions in the keeping of a dog. He never once seemed to realize she wasn't an entire stranger to domestic animals. She didn't particularly like dogs, but she was tolerant. She did understand them. At least she assumed she was understanding.

Sitting next to her and watching her, Rip knew he couldn't just stare at her. So he found things to say that allowed him to watch her as he said those things to her. He told Lu, "If somebody you don't like gets near you, the dog'll protect you. Just tell him to stay."

Tolerantly, she replied, "Okay."

"Uh. On that yearly flying checkup, what time do you think you can be out there to the place?"

"When do you have to leave?"

Rip smiled a little. "Not until about seven."

"In the *morning?*"

"No…no! In the evening. I may be a little late getting back the next night. You may have to… stay…over…again." He had some trouble with the actual words, that way.

She was dismissive, "I can drive at night. You know good and well that I can't stay the night, when you get back. My staying overnight with you would be a raw scandal!"

"*Raw!* How shocking!"

"It would be."

"Naw." He was lazy-eyed and amused. "People stay over all the time. We're a long way away from other places. The early Keepers saw to it that no town was started close by. They didn't want just anybody coming around."

"How selective."

"They are. We've got a good bunch, out at the place. You've met most of them. They're easy and they don't quarrel or complain or do anything mean."

"How…mean?"

And he replied instantly, "Like holding me off from you."

She retorted indignantly, "I've tried every which way—"

His slow, TEXAS words instantly interrupted with: "If you recall, you declined staying with me that afternoon at Hank and Marge's."

"You mean—? I didn't even think of…of… Well, darn!"

Those words turned him into mush. The road was long and empty, he pulled over and took her against his hungry body and he really kissed her. He was merciless.

She was wrecked.

Well, he was, too, almost entirely. How strange that she was a malleable mess while he was riveted. His breathing was very apparent, because his lungs had panicked, and his hands trembled while his body shivered.

His sex was rigid, shockingly alert and out of control.

Men have to deal with all sorts of problems. Women, sex, all that kinds of things. It's a hard life. But even thinking of his hard life, he was amused by his hard body. He smiled down at the swooning woman in his arms. She was his. If he could just find a place.

So on Thursday afternoon, Lu drove a rental car out to the Keepers' place. She'd gone to what passed as a deli in the town. There, she'd gone into the kitchen and the cook wouldn't let her touch anything. He was earnest. He appeared as a stoic, but he only allowed her to point. She did that and selected a picnic supper of all sorts of interesting nibbles.

She arrived at Rip's place just before five. Not very many men are too thrilled with a supper of just dainty nibbles. Not unless he hasn't had the woman and is still just anticipating. Under those circumstances, he can be quite open-minded, malleable and bending...well, mentally bending, but not too far physically.

Rip helped Lu carry in all the packages. He hesitated to inquire what all she'd brought. It was such a lot that he was a tad breathless. With all that stuff, she might be staying for several days. So while he didn't mention the boxes and suitcase, he did notice the meat packages.

It looked to Rip as if Lu was settling in for at least some time. He was exuberant. With all the packages and the suitcase inside the house, she was his. He helped her get settled.

As he helped carry her stuff inside, how many times did Rip tell Lu, "Don't let anybody in the house."

She asked, "Mrs. Keeper?"

"Nobody else."

"Mrs. Timmons?"

"Okay, but nobody else."

Lu tilted back her head and looked at Rip over her cheekbones. She inquired in a frosty manner, "Maybe you should make out a list so that I can check it if someone really comes to knock on your door."

Glad for the opening, he considered with narrowed eyes looking off to one side. He determined logically, "Any woman would probably be okay, but none of the men."

"The senior Mr. Keeper?"

"Not without his wife."

Lu sighed in a long gust and said, "Of course."

"You needn't go to the big house for supper. You can eat here."

She lifted one of the packages. "I brought us supper."

He was shocked. So that's what all those packages were? He said, "I got steaks."

She dismissed that. "We can freeze them."

His stare was stark. A steak could tide him over a long night. All that stuff in all those little wrappings were finger food and not at all filling...for a man who worked so hard that he needed a lasting meal and had the room for it.

She probably had all kinds of little taste things and curled things and one-bite things. He'd have to figure out a way to also sear the steak, or he might not survive the next couple of days.

At best, women are baffling and illogical...to men, while Lu probably wouldn't understand Rip having the steak...too. It was not logical.

Lu really didn't understand Rip wanting the steak...too.

He told her, "I need some red meat to last me...through this yearly checkout. We don't get to eat regularly as we're tested. We're tested in more ways than just flying from A to B to C. They put us through some interesting trials to see if we can handle things right."

"Who decides? What if someone does it wrong?"

He explained, "We're corrected and shown why we should have done what. We learn...more."

"Why do they do that each year?"

"To be sure we clearly remember what we've learned. It can save our necks."

Lu nodded thoughtfully as she agreed, "I can see doing that."

Rip reminded her, "People do it when they get their drivers' licenses."

"Yes." She grinned. "I hadn't remembered that."

"Your car license must be about ready to be renewed. You ought to read up on it. Then you won't say, 'Oh, I'd forgotten to do that.'"

"I'm a superb driver."

"You're automatic because you drive a lot. You forget the rules, you just do them. That's the way it is for pilots, too. With the tests, they rattle us to make sure we remember why and exactly how."

She stopped what she was doing and smiled at him. "I'm glad somebody makes you remember and do the flying right."

He told her earnestly, "I always look forward to the tests. They challenge me, and I love it."

Lu watched him for only a portion of a minute, but she saw the man. Such a man would expect a woman to match him. Could she? Did she really want to? How interesting.

It was while they were having their supper that the wind began. She was startled; he appeared to be.

She frowned at the far sky with the lightning behind the huge, piling-up, towering bunches of dark clouds. She told him firmly, "You can't possibly do your flight-testing in such weather."

He watched the sky thoughtfully and mused as if to himself, "Wonder where this came from. It wasn't on the weather maps." Then he looked at her and explained, "I'll have to call in. The phone, here, is on the blink, I'll have to go to a neighbor's house. I'll be back."

She said, "Okay."

The more dire the thundering, the higher the horizon cloud pileup, the more certain she was that Rip was *not* going to fly that night...no matter what the pilot in charge said. She'd call her uncle who was on the pilot board. He had clout. If he wasn't sure, she could convince him that Rip was not going to fly in that weather!

She took pictures of the rising, fattening, black clouds with the interesting lightning slashing among it all. And then there were the background flashes that showed the bulk and height of those serious, black clouds. She had back up if the board got suspic— became blank.

She went to the phone and picked it up. It was dead. She automatically assumed it did not work. She remembered Rip had said it was dead. Things happen out in the boondocks thisaway. She looked at the phone more carefully and saw that a switch was wrong, and she turned the phone on. How strange Rip hadn't noticed.

She called her uncle whose answering machine said he was at his club. She called there and someone fetched him from his dinner. He tried several times to interrupt, then he finally managed as he said, "Such flying was canceled two days ago when the weatherman saw how this storm was coming."

Lu said, "Oh."

Her uncle said, "Nice talking to you. Be careful of that crafty male you're with. Behave. We all love you. Tell Andrew to get out of that bed and get going."

"He's—"

But her uncle had hung up the phone. Having said what needed saying, he hadn't thought visiting was needed.

Lu looked thoughtfully at the allegedly dead but humming phone. Men are strange—and crafty. If they'd known about the storm, Rip had. Hmmmm. She slowly put the phone back into its cradle...and she reset the switch back as it'd been. Yep. That's what she did. She then smiled slyly. Women can also be clever.

Her eyes didn't slit. They were wide and so innocent that any man ought to take notice right away...and be a tad suspicious.

Rip came into the house like some bear had chased him the entire way back. He stopped with his hand still on the inside knob of the slammed door. Again the squint-wrinkles by his eyes were naked.

He said, "It's going to be a hell of a storm. I wouldn't want you to even try to get to the big house. The lightning is going to be deadly. We can sit back from the windows and watch. It'll be the Storm of the Century!"

And she said, "Well, we're right at the end of this century, so it can probably keep the title from some other pushy storm trying to outdo it."

Earnestly, he told her, "I can't get you up to the big house. Listen."

The winds had begun. The power of them was building. Nature is sometimes quite intrusively awesome. Rip had timed everything quite well.

He assimilated the facts that Lu had accepted the responsibility of her lax brother's dog, so she was there. The storm would be such that it would keep her there. She thought the phone didn't work.

He'd been sneaky and clever about the phone. He looked at her seriously. He asked, "If you want me to go out in all this—" he gestured to the sky "—I will."

How noble.

She considered him. Her eyes were just right and not even one tiny smile sneaked in to quirk her lips. She was quite clever. Then she said, "You're very brave to offer, but I can't have you risking all that lightning."

He didn't laugh. He pushed up his lower lip and tucked both lips rather severely. He managed to reply, "Yeah." And it was serious sounding. Enough so.

His eyes began to dance so he looked down at his hands like an awkward, untrained man who wasn't at all sure how to go on.

She said, "Will my car be all right in all this?"

"I put it in a garage close to here."

"Thank you." She looked at him with the right amount of gratitude, but she was thinking how he'd managed her car's disappearance so quickly. Whose garage? Which way? Who had the keys?

But then she looked at him and saw the intensity in him. He was so tense that he just about shivered. And she smiled. She said, "I'm glad that storm came along right now."

He took in a lungful of air—which showed that he'd been holding what breath he'd had—and he relaxed considerably. Since he could do that much relaxing and still be standing up okay, she knew how tense he'd been, how uncertain of her.

He earnestly lied again. He said, "This storm isn't on any of the maps."

"Oh?" That was a reply, but it wasn't the kind that made him believe she agreed with him.

So he said very seriously, "I'm sure glad you're

not out on that road, right now. I'm glad you got here.''

It was very difficult for her not to just laugh. Maybe she should. She said, ''I do hope I'm not a burden?''

''Oh, no. Don't even think that. I'm afraid of storms, and I'll be so glad not to be alone in this big one.''

She laughed out loud.

Eight

As they stood solemnly watching the approaching storm, and in a rather foggy voice, Rip told Lu, "I didn't think you was gonna get here."

Lu looked at him blankly.

He went on, "I...shaved...again." He was so earnest. His hands were in his pant pockets. He jittered.

She tilted her head and finally said, "Let me feel your—"

He almost went into overdrive with that bald—

But Lu was saying, "—face. You may be careless in shaving. I must not appear—after tonight—with whisker burn."

He said with quick earnestness, "I'm smooth as a baby's bottom. Feel me...uhhh...feel my face." His breathing had changed considerably and his eye crinkles were again exposed. But then he asked, "How'd a woman, that innocent, get to know about whisker burn?''

"Roommates in college." Lu said that as she considered him. She decided she would probably realize he was losing interest in her when he no longer looked so bare-faced and innocent.

Then she wondered: Was he an innocent? The crew lived clear out there, and there surely weren't many women around. Apparently none of the women, there, was loose.

So she asked, "Who all lives on the ranch?"

He replied with a hand wave that included a good deal of the area, "Not a whole lot."

She inquired, "Are there any young, uh, eager women out in this area?"

Watching her, Rip replied, "Naw."

Actually, in the unmarried list, there was the old washwoman who ironed shirts for the crew. Her name was Miz Bender. The guys washed their clothes at the laundry room, but only one guy ironed his own shirts. Another just wore his shirts wrinkled. It didn't matter to him or the herds.

Rip was having it tough. A man starts out wanting a woman, any woman, then he realizes he just wants A woman. Her. He had targeted The One. Could she want him? For how long? That was the touchy part.

Lu seemed to just be interested in tasting him out of curiosity. She hadn't seemed to be a tease who just liked stirring a man to the peak until she would soothe him—or to walk on off, leaving Rip in a fit.

Then his eyes were startled as he remembered his visit to the drugstore for condoms. The happening was a serious clue to Rip. He had not noticed *any* woman in that whole, *entire* store! Now that was sobering. Men noticed women. Lu had blinded him to other women? He was caught?

No. Of course not. Rip wasn't ready to settle down. Not yet. Lu admitted she was determined to taste her first man before she went back to East TEXAS. Rip just wanted to get Lu as soon as he could, before she took off. So he was anxious. But he did know, for her first time, there had to be some preliminaries.

She was almost willing. She wasn't leaning her soft, interesting body against him and smiling up into his face with her mouth available. She hadn't rubbed her…body…against…his…

Just thinking the words, he didn't breathe right. He was noisy. He shuddered like a serious quake. He just about went into overdrive.

But he knew he had to be patient. He wanted it to be good for her. When it was all over, he wanted her to smile and slowly blink her eyes at him. He wanted her to stretch and yawn, as she turned her body for him. He'd heard men talking about women doing that like lazy, sleepy cats.

Lu said, "I'll put out the food."

Food? Food! Who wanted…food? He wasn't hungry for *food!* But he said, "I'll help."

That was to show Lu that Rip was mature and logical. That he wasn't entirely lost in sex. He could function. He understood what *else* there was in life besides sex. There was… Well, there was…

Rip looked blank as he watched the magic woman. He forgot what he was doing, but whatever it was, it wasn't what he wanted to be doing.

So Lu put out the food carefully from the various

odd little wrappings and tiny paper bags. She had all sorts of strange nibbles.

Rip looked at them with suspicion.

Any man wants— Well, if he's going to eat, he wants something solid like a seared steak, a baked potato and beer. The steak and potato were meat and a vegetable. He'd soothe it down to his stomach as he drank the beer made from hops, which are good nutrition.

Rip watched with suspicion as Lu removed things from the strange little bags and unwrapped other things. There were slices of meats so thin that you could see through them. Why so thin? There were things wrapped in such coverings that looked very questionable. Rip narrowed his eyes.

He asked Lu, "Where'd you get this...stuff." It wasn't a question. There was no way such finger-sized things could be labeled as food.

She said, "Try this."

And she had the guts to hold something suspicious up for his mouth to taste it from her fingers. How could he refuse? If he said, "Naw!" and pulled back, she could be offended and that would blow the whole, entire ball of wax!

He looked at her as if she was probably disguised from being the Wicked Witch of the West in *The Wizard of Oz* which he saw at a very vulnerable age. Actually, she looked like a princess, but she was holding that cursed whatever for him to—eat.

A man has to do a whole lot of things that he doesn't want to do. He has to clean stables, kill known and loved horses that have splintered legs...and eat strange, questionable things some just-about-willing female holds for him to taste.

The greater part of his body went into shock. It was negative. His sex was single-minded. Only his brain stayed clear enough that it could say to his mouth: Eat it.

The things a man does for a woman would boggle any ordinary brain. But a time comes, when pleasing a woman takes primary status, and he was very shocked and breathing oddly in panic as his mouth opened on some command. Probably her eyes had caused him to obey.

Lu opened her own mouth as she popped the tidbit into his. She closed her own soft lips and smiled.

He wasn't sure if he should refrain from actually swallowing that stuff, or just go ahead and do it. While he decided, his taste buds became alert and were pleased! So he knew that something pleasant had covered the deadly stomach cramping stuff that was underneath it.

Rip figured that if he didn't chew, the tidbit might just go on through his body without harming him. So he carefully swallowed in some dread.

She scolded, "You didn't chew it!"

He was distracted in feeling that bit all the way to his tender stomach which was vital to his life. So he didn't know exactly what she protested, and he just nodded.

She tilted her head from side to side in pretended annoyance. Her frown was canceled by her grinning mouth. She said, "Okay, sailor, try this. But this time, *chew* it!"

And she lifted another kind of tidbit and held it for him to taste.

How come she wasn't eating any of the strange, weird stuff? She was just pushing them onto him! So he took up a similar looking something rolled in some of the transparent meat, and he said, "Your turn," like he was being a gentleman.

A man just must be sure he's in charge. He can't be lured into disaster by some pure-looking Lorelei, the mermaid who sings in the sea and lures sailors to her...to be carried to the bottom of the sea, by her, and gradually drowned.

Instead of drowning him, she was feeding him suspicious things. He'd just see if she'd eat any.

Lu took the proffered wicked bit sweetly between her lips and she smiled as she did that.

He watched her eat it, chewing. He didn't wipe off his fingers on his trousers, but he would have liked washing his entire hands in a lye soap. He waited to see if she would swallow that suspicious stuff...and, by golly, she did!

She smiled at him and said, "We have another of those. They are delicious!"

He doubted that.

Women can waste more time! If she wanted to eat, why didn't they just go ahead and...eat? The storm was nearing their place. The sounds cracked and boomed. The sky was so dark that it was an early night. The winds moaned and whistled around the buildings and shrieked through the trees.

It was really something. Rip's ears were caught up by the wild sounds outside. As he automatically went around opening the windows an inch from the top and bottom to stabilize the pressure, he wondered if there was anything he could do to help the ranch. The planes were already in the shelters and tied down. But the animals—

He ought to call in and see if he was needed. He looked at Lu with somber eyes. He might have to be away from the place after all.

Then he recalled that he had deliberately put the phone out of order. It appeared not to work. If he was to keep her thinking he was an honest, simple man—as he'd seemed—he could not use the supposedly dead phone.

Well, if he was needed, somebody would come by the house—and he'd be in bed with her? Interrupted? Good gravy, what a mess that would be. He'd probably strangle the guy who interrupted them!

So.

They might just as well eat and wait out the storm. The things a man has to do in this life are awesomely severe and trying to his soul.

Not only the phone didn't work, with good reason, but the lights went out. The storm was building remarkably. He told her, "We'd better have supper. We may have to spend the night in the cyclone cellar."

She wasn't at all rattled. She said, "That will be interesting." She didn't blink or gasp. She accepted that the storm could be not only awesome…but dangerous.

It was then that he began to see what other talents Lu might have besides poker and maybe sex. She was Andrew's sister, so the fact that she wasn't afraid of storms might not be all that surprising. The Parsons could all well be a bit strange. Again, Rip observed Lu a little differently.

So they arranged their supper. Lu was absolutely charming. In the candlelight and carrying a flashlight, they fixed the table. He noted that she did flinch with the distant crashing of lightning-caused thunder. The streaking slash flashing of lightning and the following boom! They were deep sounds. Serious sounds. Earnest, deadly sounds.

Rip turned on the emergency light which was dim. Anyone in the room could see where there were chairs, if there was a dog or cat in the way, or if there was another person close by.

But his attention narrowed. There was Lu. He just looked at her with his bare eyes.

She was alert but she wasn't at all tilted by the Storm. This one couldn't just be *a* Storm. It was a *storm!* It was such that people would use it to compare any other storm to this one. None of the coming ones would measure up to this one. There'd be arguments. It would be stimulating.

Joe's wife would probably choose that night to have their baby. Women did that kind of thing. Poor Joe. He'd have a hell of a night.

Rip pulled the shades down so Lu wouldn't be bombarded by seeing the streaks of lightning. He couldn't have her that scared.

He began to worry about her safety. This was one hell of a Storm of the Century.

The dog was alert. He didn't flinch or whine or anything. He was simply interested. He was a lot like the humans in the Parsons family. Well, not their absent father who was even stranger.

The kids must take after their mother. Now that was interesting to figure. But their mother had sounded thataway on the phone. She'd sounded…free. Rip looked over at the flowering woman who lured him so painfully. She was just like her brother!

Well, she was more logical. Maybe. Who'd talked to her brother? He was sly and pretended to be out of touch. It takes talent to endure every day of faking it. But he was awake all night long. Hmmm. His sister was more open. That was the difference.

She was logical. She viewed things openly and commented. She wanted Rip. But she'd put a limit on how long she would want him.

Her attitude of limit kind of saddened Rip. He looked at her with his bare eyes and saw her as a jewel. If she cottoned to him and stayed around, she would take him over, watching over him, feeding him strange things from her fingers and she'd probably ruin him altogether.

But she would want him around— No, she only wanted a taste of him. She'd said that. And she planned to go away and leave him there, alone, used and abandoned. He sighed sadly.

She didn't notice.

Buddy went to the window and put his nose under the shade to stretch up and watch out beyond.

That very action proved the dog wasn't cowed, at all. The towering clouds were awesome. But slowly ballooning that way with the lightning flashing and letting a body see what was coming, was a little rude.

It was a show-off thing done by the probably bored gods of the weather.

As with any person who might have to be away from the place, out in his plane or truck and doing something boring, like fixing a clipped fence, Rip had a radio that didn't depend on wires or plugs. He turned it to the weather station.

The speaker was saying, "...now. You all'd better get yourselves to shelter. It's gonna be something else than what we're used to. Good lu—" And he went off the air.

Whoever heard of the weather station just going off the air like that?

So Rip turned to the flight station who told them who was up—and where—in a code of their own. "—yeah. So get under cover. If you're stupid enough not to know about this Storm, hear me now. Get away. Get out of there. Don't try to fly through it. It'll tear you apa—"

Rip turned to Lu. "We need to go downstairs to the shelter."

And on cue, the house began to tremble. How strange to hear the furniture on the bare floors jiggle with the echoing thunder. But the two humans jiggled, too.

He saw that her breasts shimmered. How could he be so sexually stricken in such a horrendous time? How could his libido intrude into this alarm to get her to safety?

Rip wanted to get her somewhere safe—first. Surely he wouldn't just take her down on the throw rug by the door? He wrestled with that idea and organized his thoughts to what else was pushing. He blew out all the candles. She helped.

Being part cat, and a pilot to boot, Rip reached out and took Lu's hand. He told her brother's dog, "Come!" He'd never ordered Andrew's dog before, so Rip was rather startled that Buddy obeyed immediately.

Of course, the dog had been looking out the window at the storm, and Andrew's dog was most certainly not an idiot.

As Rip tugged Lu across the shivering floor toward the door down to the cyclone cellar, Lu asked, "Do you have any condoms with you?"

Although he nodded in reply, Rip was shocked that such a fragile, well-behaved woman would ask such a question at such a time of alarm. It made him wonder a little if it was he who was the seducer...or she? Maybe he ought to wait a trifle and find out?

He was not waiting the first time. He was quite positive about that. He'd allow her to coax him the rest of the times. She could even lure him. Yes!

So they got down the stairs to the cyclone shelter. It was under the west side of the house. Most TEXAS storms came from the west. Hurricanes came from the east, but the ranch was far enough inland that they survived those.

With the cyclone cellars being on the west, if the house was knocked over by something like a bad storm, then the house wouldn't fall on top of the shelter and trap them. The house would be torn off toward the east, and those in the shelter could get out.

There were times when the storms were so berserk that they whirled around and hit the east side of the house. But there were enough people around, in that area, to dig entrapped others out.

And they had the oaks. The oaks stood firm. Their roots went deep and their branches were strong. They also protected the houses from the winds. The trees broke the rush of the storms.

Who all has seen the oaks' great waving limbs in a wind that matches ninety miles an hour? A hundred ten miles. The tree branches didn't have that much practice in moving. How can those seldom disturbed, big limbs wave, thataway, and stay on the trunk without cracking off? It is a wonder.

Oak trees are precious but they take forever to grow. That's probably why they're so stubborn.

The two humans carried flashlights as they crept down the stairs to the shelter. Buddy could see without that help, so the dog just went on ahead. He quite swiftly inspected the area to be sure there were no rats or snakes or lurking murderers.

The sound of the storm was ear catching. And being in the cellar, that way, made them almost too isolated. Lu said, "I think I'd rather be able to see what is going on."

"Not this time."

So she sassed, "Which time can I do that?"

"Did you hear what the radio guy said just before the contact was broken?"

She was logical. "The storm isn't yet here. Let's go out and see what's happening."

Rip began to smile. "Okay. But if I think we need to come back, you don't argue—at all."

She smiled but tucked her lips so that she might

minimize it. Her eyes danced with excitement. She said quickly, "I promise."

Oddly enough, the dog was as eager to get outside, and look, as either of the two people. Buddy crowded them and was out first. The great milling clouds were closer, higher, darker. How strange the storm took as long as it did to move. The roiling black clouds were towering. But the storm wasn't in any kind of a forward rush.

It was rather as if the storm was saying, "Look what's coming! Get under cover."

The flashes of lightning allowed the watchers to see that around the ranch there were other people outside their distant houses. No one was out far and away from shelter that the two watchers could see.

If others had gone on out farther, they were not apparent, but the storm surely was. If any of the people got out too far, and were in danger, their stupidity would tip the searchers' tempers quite a bit. Nobody could ignore the approaching, towering danger.

Then came the old World War II siren giving further alarm to the size of the storm. The alarm had come in handy more than once. They were convinced whatever was coming, was serious.

With the ground wind rising, Rip took hold of Lu's arm. She allowed that. He didn't take the dog's collar or even tell the dog to stay. By then, Rip knew the dog understood danger quite clearly.

Did Lu?

Rip's eyes slid over to her. Her soft dress was pressed against her body so that her body was only concealed in a fake cloth skin. Her form was imprinted by the wind. She was something. She wasn't wearing a bra.

Rip didn't need an additional lure, he was already triggered. He considered that if she was in a hooded cape, he'd be attracted to her.

He thought one lure might be her attention to everything. She was so curious about anything. She moved her head. She stretched her neck. She was alert and interested.

It wasn't just the storm that caught her attention. She was thataway about everything. She was one hell of a card player. She was competitive. A man would have to be alert, or she'd discard him as dull.

He told her, "To fly in a plane above something like that—" He gestured at the dark blue and black, roiling clouds with the stagelike back lightning. "It's exciting and fascinating. You just want to go along and watch."

"Did you?"

He lowered his eyes to her. "I stuck with the storm. I watched until I had only enough gas to get back." And he knew he would do the same kind of thing with Lu. She fascinated him.

She was probably as dangerous to him as such a storm was to trees and houses. He knew he'd stay with her as long as she let him. As long as he could.

His face was so serious that Lu asked, "Are you okay? Is this storm bothering you? Were all the flyers told about it in time?"

And he told her the truth. "I was told two days ago. I wanted you with me. I thought if you knew I'd be here, there was no reason for you to be with the dog. I tricked you into coming out here and now you're trapped."

She nodded with her lower lip out. "I can't tell you how pleased I am that you want me that much. You must be desperate."

"Aren't you?"

"If you recall, I've been trying for some time to find us a place to be. Wasn't this seduction all my own making? Were you already willing?"

He lifted his head slowly and brought it down equally slow. He said, "Yes."

"Oh, good! Now you can take all the burden of craft onto your back, and I'll be free to just enjoy you."

He told her, against the shrill wind which he hadn't even noticed, "I've heard it's kinda rough the first time for a lady. They tell me it isn't that tough for a guy."

Her eyes widened in disbelief. "You're a virgin...too?"

"Don't be so surprised," he protested with indignation. "You've seen how it is out here. What did you expect? Somebody...trained?" Men can be very indignant and huffy at just the right time.

She gasped. Then she frowned. "Just don't give up too soon, okay?"

He coughed discreetly to cover his surprised laugh. He urged, "Be careful with me. Don't get rough."

Lu became quite serious. "I've read up." She put a kind hand on his arm and reassured him gently. "I know what we need to do and how." She was so earnest. She told him, "Don't be afraid."

Rip loved it. Very urgently, he said, "Don't just jump me. One of the guys told about that happening to him. He thought she was trying to get his paycheck out of his pocket."

"Awwww."

And Rip told Lu earnestly, "Men out here aren't very—"

She put her arm over her eyes and said, "The dust!"

He hadn't noticed the storm was closer. The dust was swirled around and wild. They ought not to be outside in this— He said, "Let's go in—"

And she was at the door saying, "Hurry!"

But *he* said, "Get inside before it rains and your clothes will keep some of the moisture from getting on the dirt." It was the usual TEXAS comment when it rains. This was also said in torrential downpours. TEXANS just say that sort of thing.

Of course, Buddy got inside first. The damned dog almost trampled Lu, and that made Rip swat him. He told the dog, "By golly, you can be a gentleman and wait your turn!"

Without any hostility, the dog looked at Rip with interest and no understanding at all. Buddy was exactly like his master, Andrew Parsons, with only himself to care about. With Buddy, he monitored Andrew, but the dog felt he was next to Andrew in the scale of living.

Or—

The dog had had it thataway until Rip just showed him there were other beings after Andrew. It was the woman. Now that was interesting to Buddy. He observed the woman and realized she was very similar to her brother. She was just more subtle.

Buddy took the indication, so firmly given by the man called Rip, that he was to protect the woman also. Now that was interesting. Buddy hadn't noticed any particular reason for doing that. However, she had once shared a bed with him. So far, he'd had no particular trouble sleeping on a bed with humans.

While it was something of a surprise, the dog was stimulated by having another person to protect. It gave him something to do. Andrew being in the hospital was really quite boring. Buddy had talked to his man called Andrew to keep him up on what was going on, but Buddy never received any cognizant replies.

For some reason, the man called Rip put Buddy out of the shelter. That had delighted the dog. He went up the stairs, used his teeth to pull the shades a tad and let each of them snap to the top of the window. Then he went under the table and watched. The storm was fascinating.

Meanwhile, down in the basement, the isolation, the probability of anyone intruding nil, the couple looked at each other with some intensity.

She smiled just the littlest bit, but her eyes sparkled and her breaths were quicker. She was interested.

His breathing was becoming harsh. Men are so obvious. His hands trembled and he looked at her with his naked eyes. He said, "You're really something."

"Something... Now what do you mean by that?" She grinned in a teasing manner.

The invitation to ease himself with banter went right by him because he didn't actually hear what Lu said, he was so concentrated.

Men tend to have tunnel vision, and right then, Rip's whole, entire attention was on her.

Nine

The still-distant, awesome storm was carefully approaching. It was like the coming of an unknown structure of war that was startling in its size. To see the roiling storm clouds, a fragile human had to tilt back his head just to see the approaching tops of the lightning's revelation of the threatening mass.

In that section of the TEXAS tablelands, the people were seeing it all happen. To most of the witnesses, it was fascinating. People can be strange in their choices of personal observations.

Those who were appalled by the storms, and mentioned it, were somewhat ignored. With a rather irritating lack of attention, their hands were patted...their arms, or backs or heads, depending on who they were, how tall and how old.

And there was a very small section of people who

were simply indifferent about a change in the weather
for one reason or another. A…What will Be, will
Be—kind of attitude. Rip and Lu were two of that
scattered group.

The two beings of opposite gender had gone out
and looked at the piled threatening mass in the sky.
Lu had not really assimilated what was happening in
the weather. And Rip only looked at the advancing,
towering clouds from a flyer's point of view through
diligent practice. To him, in that area, it was not flying
weather.

They were distracted from The Storm by their interest in sex. How basic.

Lu was a little tense. But her reaction was not with
the approaching storm, it was about Rip. She'd heard
talk of guys wanting sex right away and being very
quick. After their release, instead of trapping the female under them, the males flopped off to one side
of their partner, with some courtesy, and then went
into a dead sleep.

Men are really very basic.

The females, who'd reported this in single-sex
gatherings of the female variety, were disgruntled and
disgusted. It had been a warning.

In the shelter, Lu slid out of most of her clothing,
leaving her slip on so that, no matter what all he did,
at least her tummy button would be covered and she
wouldn't feel so—well—naked.

Rip's breathing was rather harsh. He stripped in no
time at all. His disrobing was a little brag and a little
self-confidence in his muscular body. He claimed his
muscles had been achieved solely by being overworked to a standstill, by the Keepers.

All the hands said that same thing—about being worked to the very bone. It wasn't true. The Keepers tended to indulge the crew. Their tolerance and patience was how come the crew could complain with such elaborate drama.

With Rip disrobing in that quick way, Lu lowered her eyelashes as if she was shy, but she actually was judging Rip.

When he slid out of his trousers along with his underwear, he did it with an odd assortment of pride, show-offiness and watchfulness. Females can be strange. A man has to counter hesitation or—

She was appalled! He was too big. It would *never* fit! The whole effort was down the drain. She flopped her hands and sighed, but she began to sit up and swing her legs off the inflated, emergency bed in that cyclone shelter.

Rip immediately understood the whole shebang. There had been male gathering discussions on just this very problem with a woman declaring a man was too big for a woman any size at all.

Making her understand that it wasn't true, was rather an ego trip for the male. A man could be exceptionally earnest immediately. Rip began as he quickly said, "It's okay. Don't let it worry you one bit. It'll fit."

She looked at him alertly, "How do you know that? Who all have you tried it on?"

Right away, he soothed her, "Guys talk. The older married guys—" he put that in pretty quick "—tell us others." He moved toward her. "See? It's harmless." His voice turned rusty. "Feel it."

She did, reaching out very carefully, with a thumb

and an opposing finger. "Why—" She gasped. "It's as hard as a rock!" Then, as his sex jumped around, she exclaimed, "It's alive!" That was in shock. She then decided firmly, "It won't fit."

She abandoned the whole idea and began to get up off the carefully inflated, emergency bed.

Panic flooded Rip's rigid body, but like any male, he soothed. "Of course, it'll work. God wouldn't have made us this-a way if it didn't."

As Rip remembered, it was his old friend, the Ox, who'd shared that response to a frightened, discarding woman.

Rip said earnestly and very, very seriously, "You gotta know that I would never in this world hurt you. I promise you, it'll be okay."

Not at all convinced, she said, "Maybe later."

His heart sank, his sex bounced in panic, he sat carefully down like a dog that has been told not to get on the bed. He talked the whole, entire time.

Again, he promised, "It'll be okay. Let's just hug each other and listen to the storm. Let's just be close together, here."

None of what he said made much sense, but he did soothe her for she figured he was intelligent enough not to try anything on her after that shock. Rip was enormous!

Rip gathered her to him and prevented his muscles from holding her too tightly and snapping a bone on her spine.

He rubbed one big, hard hand on her stomach, and it was just perfect. She gradually relaxed and sighed. He eased them back onto the inflated bed. She murmured. Her eyes closed.

Any woman likes her stomach rubbed thataway. Rip was leaning up on one elbow as his big hand moved soothingly on her stomach. It felt...wonderful.

He leaned over and his face was just about over her tummy button, he was looking at—her. That was rather shocking, and she blushed scarlet. She asked rather tersely, "Just what are you doing?"

Undistracted, he replied immediately and with some interest, "I'm looking for the tattoo of my phone number. The one you promised you wouldn't allow anybody to know. That you would tattoo it on you by yourself. It has to be on the front of you— among all this interesting different decoration you have on you. I'm looking here because I don't think you could of put it on your back." He looked at her in a fake shock. "It isn't here!"

"No."

"Well, I'll be darned." He appeared shocked. "You *said* you was gonna do it, and I *believed* you! But since you haven't called me—at all—I thought you'd mistattooed it and done the wrong number!"

Smiling a little at his appalled earnestness, and remembering how reluctant he'd been in giving her his phone number, she said, "My brother is somewhat better. He can have company."

Knowing all that, Rip said a nothing, "Yeah."

Her voice quavered a little. "I thought he was going to die."

"Naw." Rip gathered her body to him as he settled down to endure friendship and give up sex...for a while longer. Rip considered her selfish, self-centered brother. "It would take a whole lot of effort to kill off Andrew."

"He'd fight." She said that immediately.

With the heavy sounds of the winds around the house and the serious crashing of lightning, Rip was holding her soft body close in his arms and against his own, naked, rigidly fascinated body. He replied to her comment quite thoughtfully, "No. Andrew'd never do anything...so basic as fighting. He'd just be so curious, he'd drive...the attacker nuts...with his endless questions...and ponderous comments."

Andrew's sister considered that evaluation. She nodded with her head on the pillow as Rip kissed along her shoulder. She said, "Ummmm." Then she told Rip, "Well, yes. That is...very close to explaining Andrew. He is not only—ummmm, lower...a curious person to other people. He is, indeed, just a plainly...curious...person."

As Rip almost grazed along her flesh, and just before she'd given up on his half of the discussion, he had nosed aside the slip from her tummy button, he told her against her stomach, "He needs to read more." He then expanded his communication, "Most of what he searches about, has been overly searched out...and written about." And he lifted his mouth to mention, "A good library would solve all the things that Andrew explores as being new and unknown to others."

Adjusting her body so that Rip could reach some areas better, she inquired rather oddly, "Like... the...mmmmm...tableland?" she inquired.

Rip agreed. "Old stuff."

So she commented as she moved her chin up, exposing her throat to his searching mouth, "I suppose...he needs to just...read more."

Rip replied, "…ummmm," for whatever that meant. He was very engrossed in what he was doing and therefore did not reply in actual words.

Her breathing was rather noticeable. She figured it was her fear of the storm. She asked, "Uhhh… Mmmmm, the storm…that's wicked."

After his nuzzling, he inquired in a rather hoarse voice, "The…storm's…wicked?"

She gasped and swallowed. Then she replied with closed eyes, "You…are…wicked."

And again he said the nothing, "Yeah."

He kissed her, and her toes curled. She said, "Shame on…you." The last word was odd because she'd gasped with an indrawn breath.

His hands moved in their rigid, controlled way as he convinced himself yet again that she was real and not another dream. His breathy voice drew out the words, as if selecting them very carefully from a big pot, as he remembered to inquire, "Uh…what've I done—to be—ashamed about?"

She moaned just a slight dribble of sound as she closed her eyes and turned her head a little. Her mouth had a very slight smile. She said, "Ummm?"

It was obvious even to the slip-covered body—right there—which distracted Rip, that she was not too cognizant. He had her! All's he had to do was just what he was doing, and in time, she'd insist! He looked at her with hungry eyes.

She was a morsel. She was tempting and ready, if she only understood that was why she was moving her head thataway and moving her body and lifting that fascinating, now naked chest, to catch his attentions. But it was all obvious because of that little moan that slid from her lips, and her head moving as her eyes closed thataway.

She was just about ready.

She didn't know that yet—but she was.

He suspected that if he coaxed her into letting him, she would be embarrassed and shocked—and she'd cry.

Very slowly, his face became gentle. She needed time. He couldn't just sneak her. It had to be her idea. He accepted that, in the days following, he was gonna go crazy. He was gonna lose sleep and make stupid replies to partly heard questions. He'd probably wreck his plane from thinking about her instead of paying attention to what he was supposed to be doing, when all he wanted to do was…her.

It was just a good thing he was in control of his want… Well, almost. He kissed her the wanting kiss that men are so skilled in knowing just how to do. Probably the Snake in Eden taught Adam that one. It is lethal. It is unfair. It is—wonderful. It makes a man rigid, and a woman melts like hot wax.

Her hands had forgotten about keeping her slip covering her. Only her tummy button was partially covered.

But with his hairy body over hers it really didn't matter because he couldn't see her naked body while he was lying that way on top of her. Her body loved the feel of his body hairiness rubbing on her soft skin.

Rip's breathing was harsh. Was he frightened by the storm? His rock hard hands were so gentle. His kisses were getting squishier. His mouth was so sweet. She put her hands on his head and slid her fingers in his hair.

With her arms up thataway, she was very vulnerable. Her body was unguarded. His hand moved gently, pushing her puffed up breast higher. And since she was still thinking fairly rationally, she figured he wasn't actually touching her breast. His hand was just under where most of her breast had been on her ribs. Ummmhummm.

Men are sneaky.

He told her she was beautiful. If it had been dead dark, and they'd never even seen each other, and didn't know what either looked like he would have still said it at that time. It's an opening-of-the-knees beginning. Men are born with that sentence locked in their heads...the one on their neck.

She began to breathe and squirm a little. She was getting restless. She was ready. She moved her shoulders. That was encouraging, but she lifted her chest to his. She breathed as if her restless legs didn't know what to do. And her hands moved to the backs of his shoulders to get him closer. Her head moved, her eyes were closed and her mouth moaned softly.

Now, how'd she know to do that?

With that telltale sound, he just practiced breathing which was hoarse and sounded quite like some distressed, bull animal.

Well, he was.

His body was already as close to hers as it could get. Only one thing wasn't where it was supposed to be. And he got scared. Almost panicked. Should he? And about berserk, he thought: Why not?

So he very carefully opened her knees and lay his hips between her thighs. His sex about went entirely wild. It was just a wonder it didn't explode.

He told her, "It'll be okay."

That was the other sentence men have in their brains, at birth. It's used under many different circumstances, depending on what is happening. Men say it on battlefields, in storms, when kids are sick, whenever it's needed. It's a handy sentence because the listener believes it.

So hearing what Rip had said, she slowly, jerkily relaxed and waited tensely for whatever he was going to do, and she would just see if it really was going to be okay. If it wasn't, she'd know that he'd lied…and as her brain went on avidly, he slowly, slowly sank into her, his body shivering with his rigid control.

It is a terrible time for a man, if he cares about the woman. The wanting, the worry the first time will hurt her, as he dealt with the rampant need so rigidly controlled.

Her eyes were quite large and they moved in quick darts as she said, "Uff!" and her body flinched.

Of course, he was instantly paralyzed. He lifted his head and looked at her face with some anxiety. Men have it tough.

She was—thoughtful. She looked up at him and said, "How strange."

That really isn't exactly what a man wants to hear at a time like that.

It was a wonder he didn't just shrivel up and quit.

But his compassion for her slowed him and, because of that, he could last long enough to catch her attention—and her pleasure.

The amazing thing was that her juices began to flow and lubricate her—and his condom. Her breathing changed. Her body became interested. Her breaths altered. Her hands moved on his back, pressing him to her. She made little, relishing sounds.

That pointed his ears, rattled his brain and riveted his body. His breathing became a little hoarse. He sought to control himself, to slow down.

But she got out of hand. She went wild! She gasped and wrapped her heels behind his knees and she rode him upside down!

He went right along, keeping up with her wild, erotic ride, and they thundered into a climax right along with the outside crash of the storm. Their storm was equal to the one outside. Theirs had been phenomenal!

The two, of opposite gender, collapsed into a boneless heap. Still locked together, and with their breathing so obvious, they didn't even hear the roar of the serious storm above the house.

His breathing was hoarse and his body was not only collapsed but entirely useless. With great effort, he moved to take some of his weight from her, but he stayed coupled.

He managed to move his hand to smooth back her hair from her face. Her hair wasn't blinding her since she was on the bottom. Her eyes were closed. However, there was that tiny smile on her sweet, swollen lips.

The smile soothed the anxiety inside the, now, only semigreedy man. She was all right. Then he looked again at that smile. It was smug! And he laughed. Helplessly, he laughed. He said, ''You liked it.''

She minimally slid open sly eyes and asked, "When can we do it again?"

In a tiny, lousy attempt at terror, he whispered, "Help! Help!"

She asked with open eyes and concern, "Would you mind?"

Energy began to pump into his sex. How rude and eager it was. He was—well—maybe just a tad embarrassed, but he was mostly smug. He said, "You animal." But his eyes danced with his delight.

She tilted her head and looked around. She told him, "I'll keep you in here and— Don't weep and complain, I'll give you a TV and food and any magazine you'd like as I—"

He said, "Okay."

She sighed and looked off to the side as she ground out, "You're supposed to plead and protest and only gradually give up. You're acting just like a sex fiend who wants to be used!"

He frowned as he considered that by tilting up his chin and looking around. Then he said, "Oh, okay."

She moved, indicating that he should.

He carefully showed off his strength by pushing up with his arms to lift his body from her. He held himself above her to look at her face. It was male domination. Genetic. She was in his control. He slowly slid from her and lay beside her.

She turned and leaned over him. "How come I never did this before now? It was terrific! Thank you."

SHE was thanking HIM? He watched her. "It was paradise." Then he added, "I was told it was."

"So this is your first time, too? How'd you know to get the condom and how to put it on?"

He lied, "I've been practicing ever since I first saw you in Andrew's room."

"That quick?"

Very seriously, in a vulnerable voice, he told her, "You're magic."

"How'd you know that?"

He frowned as if to remember. "That nurse that was teaching Andrew to move? She was good-looking and—wait a minute and listen! But she wasn't you. I didn't watch her. I watched you."

When Lu had gradually relaxed back against Rip, she mentioned thoughtfully, "That nurse is really something. Do you suppose her hair is really red?"

And HE asked innocently, "I thought she was blond...sort of dishwasher blond."

Lu smiled a little. "You're sly."

His replying smile was contented—for a while—and he hugged her soft, lax, fascinatingly naked body to his alert, naked side. He sighed in contentment. He smiled at her. It was a possessive smile.

She leaned over him a trifle and put her hands in his hair. She said, "You are good-looking."

He'd accepted that some years back. He told her, "Naw. I'm just another guy. But you're magic."

She laughed in contentment and said, "I'm very ordinary."

So he explained, "You only think that because you are magic. You think that's normal. That everybody should be magic or peons, one way or the other. How come you allowed this peon to love you?"

She replied, "Well, I did tell you that I'll be going

back East soon now, and I'll never see you again. You're a chance encounter. I do thank you for doing this for me. But I want to spread my wings and find other adventures.''

''No. You're finished with exploring. You're settling down here, with me, and learning to be a wife.''

''I am?''

''Yeah.''

She said thoughtfully, ''How shocking! I doubt seriously that I'm ready to settle down. Are you sure you are? If this was your first time, too, then maybe you want to taste some of the other women before you become nailed down by me.''

''I have the spike to nail you. You be careful how you talk, or you'll find out exactly what I mean.''

''That again.''

So, what with one thing and another, the lovers really didn't much notice The Storm of the Century. There were other humans equally distracted by unexpected free time with no interruptions.

Buddy was still upstairs, still under the dining-room table and fascinated by the uproar and violence of the storm. He watched it all out of the snapped up window shades and he was not the least afraid. He'd been through so much with Andrew that he could handle anything.

Then, too, there was that handy swinging dog door beside the front door. There was his water dish and the food dish. He was independent and free. He had no responsibilities. Andrew was under another care entirely.

*   *   *

So with the slow-moving storm, the two in the cyclone shelter had the time to get to know each other
even more intimately. They loved. That means that
they not only had sex, but they had the time to make
love together. They talked and laughed and loved in
those hours that, out beyond, were so wild and wicked
and destructive.

None of the oak trees on the Keeper place *was*
harmed unduly. There was a smaller branch here and
there that had been torn from the selfish, resisting
oaks, but that was all. Those trees had been around
so long and had such deep roots that they were adjusted to mean weather, droughts, rain, whatever
came along. They survived.

So actually, it wasn't until the next day that the
two in the cyclone cellar emerged and looked around.
They'd had stored foods and water in the cellar.
They'd talked and eaten and laughed and made love.
He had controlled his greediness. It had been a trial
for him, but he had been careful of her. He thought
three times, in a lax day thataway, was stingy, but all
right.

As they went up the stairs to the first floor, the dog
met them with a tilted, judging head. The rain was
pouring down like it was from a continual series of
buckets.

Both people talked to the dog, and Rip rubbed the
dog's back. Buddy's water was low in his bowl, and
the food was gone. Rip looked at the dog, "Mice got
your food?"

The dog laughed.

In the bath, Rip showed Lu the shower and how to work it. She asked, "We can't run out into the rain? We could take the soap with us."

"Everybody here has binoculars?" The TEXAS questioning statement. "We can't do that."

"How rigid."

Gently, watching her, he mentioned, "You can shower here. We have lots of water."

She was so glad to see the shower. She felt a tad grungy. But she was more shocked when she was showering, and Rip got in with her! He was very efficient. He washed her hair and his fingers rubbed her scalp like he'd have done to her brother's dog.

Then she wondered if he'd bathed the dog in the shower stall? But it was sparkling clean. She gave him tolerant looks as he rubbed soap all over her. In some places, his soapy hands took forever to get it done.

He noted that her black eyelashes didn't run. They were naturally black. And she was glorious in her nakedness. He began to plot how he could keep her thataway...there and naked.

So, of course, if he could wash her, then she would do him. He blushed! She loved it and her eyes twinkled.

He said, "You animal."

And she agreed in such a salacious manner.

He told her, "You shouldn't use me thisaway. I'm a nice, young man who is pure."

Her laugh was in her throat and very soft.

And he was justifiably indignant, "Until you got here, I *was!*"

She just smiled at him.

She made the back of his tongue clack in his throat, and his regard for her was so gentle. He held her to his naked body there under the shower and he groaned.

She asked carefully, "Did it fall off?"

"Not yet."

The rain went on for two more days. Unstopping. Lu stayed at Rip's place with the dog as a needless guard. Rip went out and opened dikes, and rerouted water flow. He helped find lost horses, moved cattle out of water-logged fields mostly of cotton, and reset fences.

One of the things, at a place like that, is there is *always* something to do!

But the plus part of Rip's toiling was that he came back to a house that held—her. He stood under the waterspout with his hat off and allowed the mud to be washed from him. Then he went onto the porch. And the dog pranced with welcome. So the dog got the first greeting from Rip.

And there she was. And she was real! That sweet woman—

She said, "Don't you *dare* come inside dripping wet that way. Here, I'll hold the blanket for you and you just get yourself out of those rank, wet clothes!"

He was shocked. "You're a sex fiend? You lust for my poor, tired, calf-wrecked body? You aren't one bit compassionate, I've—"

"You're hurt?" She was aghast.

Being quick, he put his hand to his forehead. "Just...a...bit. We had to get a stuck calf out of the mud."

She scoffed, "There's only rocks up here on the tableland."

Rip shook his head from side to side in chiding. "We don't grow cotton in rocks."

So his clothes were dropped in a gentle splat to the porch floor, and he looked at Lu with an exhausted longing. Could he? He'd probably go to sleep right on top of her. He smiled at the idea of sleeping with his sex so wondrously embedded.

She didn't even suggest getting into bed with him. She turned on the shower and felt it with her wrist as she scolded him for killing himself over a damned *calf!*

But she didn't get into the shower with him.

People began to call and ask how "...you all are." Only non-Southerners call one person "you all" so EVERYbody knew she'd been with Rip since before the storm.

With the calls, Rip told Lu, "Well, hell, I guess in order to save my reputation—"

"*Your* reputa—"

"—we'll just have to shack up."

Gradually, she began to laugh.

So it was that two days later the storm was over. No creature on the place had died.

The two new lovers went up to the big house and gave their greetings to the Keepers. And the Keepers said Lu should come stay with them! Tom Keeper laughed while Rip just drew in a shocked breath.

But Lu told the Keepers, "Thank you, but we're having an affair."

Rip's ears got red, but he grinned and controlled the grin.

Mrs. Keeper said with a marked lack of shock, "How shocking."

And Lu mentioned casually, "We'll probably get married. He's very structured."

The time did pass. Lu seemed to settle in quite well. It didn't bother her at all that she was the prime study of the gossips. She drove Rip's pickup to the hospital to see her brother, and it was she who took Buddy along.

When Rip got his phone bill, he inquired of Lu, "You call your mama the day of the storm?"

She replied readily, "No. I called my uncle who is high enough in the echelon to know what's going on in flying. I asked him about canceling flying, and he told me that had been done two days before."

"Oh." Then Rip's smile began. "But you stayed anyway."

"Yep."

And he repeated an easy, smiling, "Oh."

*   *   *   *   *

Wondering what happened to Andrew? Well, his story, along with more fantastic tales of the Keeper family, is coming your way in June—from Silhouette Desire! You won't want to miss THE HARD-TO-TAME TEXAN.

DIANA PALMER
ANN MAJOR
SUSAN MALLERY

RETURN TO WHITEHORN

In **April 1998** get ready to catch the bouquet. Join in the excitement as these bestselling authors lead us down the aisle with three heartwarming tales of love and matrimony in Big Sky country.

A very engaged lady is having second thoughts about her intended; a pregnant librarian is wooed by the town bad boy; a cowgirl meets up with her first love. Which Maverick will be the next one to get hitched?

Available in **April 1998.**

Silhouette's beloved **MONTANA MAVERICKS** returns in Special Edition and Harlequin Historicals starting in February 1998, with brand-new stories from your favorite authors.

Round up these great new stories at your favorite retail outlet.

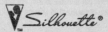

Look us up on-line at: http://www.romance.net   PSMMWEDS

Take 4 bestselling love stories FREE
Plus get a FREE surprise gift!

BEVERLY BARTON

Continues the twelve-book series— 36 Hours—in April 1998 with Book Ten

NINE MONTHS

Paige Summers couldn't have been more shocked when she learned that the man with whom she had spent one passionate, stormy night was none other than her arrogant new boss! And just because he was the father of her unborn baby didn't give him the right to claim her as his wife. Especially when he wasn't offering the one thing she wanted: his heart.

For Jared and Paige and *all* the residents of Grand Springs, Colorado, the storm-induced blackout was just the beginning of 36 Hours that changed *everything!* You won't want to miss a single book.

Available at your favorite retail outlet.

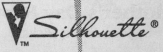